T0149447

Miracle on Mirror Lake

Mac Carroll

iUniverse LLC
Bloomington

MIRACLE ON MIRROR LAKE

iUniverse books may be ordered through booksellers or by contacting:

iUniverse LLC
1663 Liberty Drive
Bloomington, IN 47403
www.iuniverse.com
1-800-Authors (1-800-288-4677)

ISBN: 978-1-4917-2453-8 (sc)
ISBN: 978-1-4917-2452-1 (e)

Library of Congress Control Number: 2014902600

Printed in the United States of America.

iUniverse rev. date: 03/28/2014

Dedication

This book is dedicated to my lovely wife, Carol, who is forever my sweetheart, best friend, and soul mate. She believed in me when few others did, and was willing to give me a second chance in life.

Acknowledgments

I would like to start by thanking my dear wife, Carol, for having to put up with me during the many times I read her parts of my manuscript, described certain scenes, and gave her a daily report on the progress of the book. She graciously listened and supported me throughout the thick and thin of the entire process. You are the greatest!

I express my heartfelt appreciation to my loyal investors for taking a chance on this first time author; namely my four beautiful sisters, Paula, MaryAnn, Barbara and Donna. I am also grateful to my cousins, Dennis and James; as well as my two very dear friends, John and Dennis. Without them, I'd never have approached any publisher with my manuscript.

Finally, I thank the creative, dedicated, and hard-working staff at iUniverse, who made the publication process a joy more than a task. Particularly, I am grateful To Kate Van Zant, my senior publishing consultant, Dianne Lee, the Supervisor of Operations, May Alvarez, the publishing services associate, Alison Holen of the design team, George NeDeff, my editorial consultant, and finally, Brian Hallbarer from the Marketing Department, who did a superb job setting up my website.

Thank you, one and all, for without you there would be no miracle in my life.

Author's Note

The main character of my book, Adam Tiller, upon reflecting on his life-changing experience in the northern woods of Wisconsin concluded that *everyone needs to look into a mirror during their life*, or in other words to make a self-inventory and decide if he is happy with what he sees. Such introspection would hopefully lead the person to change and bring meaning to their life, happiness, and fulfillment.

There comes a time in the life of most of us, when we need to be redeemed or at least given a second chance. I am one of those people, and it is for people like you and me that I wrote this book.

Sadly, not every person in need of a second chance in life is going to get one for it hinges on one's unique set of circumstances. However, for those who have seen their reflection in the mirror, and make the best of their second chance; you know as well as I that it is the most wonderful and liberating feeling on the face of the earth.

If you are in need of a second chance, or believe that you are in need of a change in your life that will bring the meaning, happiness, and fulfillment that has been lacking; all you have to do is to stand in front of your mirror and ask, "Am I happy with what I see?" This is the first and most important step of your redemption. It is never too late to start living.

Contents

Chapter One

A Change of Scenery

*A*dam Tiller was a multi-millionaire who amassed a fortune writing detective novels. He decided to go to Mirror Lake in the hope of writing a novel in a different literary genre, even though sixteen of his twenty-two novels were *New York Times* best sellers. His fictional character, Allan Spalding, a detective in the homicide division of the Philadelphia Police Department known for his toughness, keen intellect, but also for his unorthodox methods and sexy women, had far surpassed the notoriety of Holmes, Poirot, Reacher, and Cross. He had become the *Father of Fictional Sleuths.*

Despite his success in writing, he was bored with his main character, as well as the plots involving the Philly mob, sociopaths, serial killers, drugs, sex, and the usual suspects that make their way into contemporary detective stories. He longed to create something new, more imaginative, and engaging to his readers. He didn't want to end up like many of the actors in Hollywood, who were stuck with the same screen role over and over again. He wanted to be like Sly Stallone, who shook off the role of the underdog fighter, Rocky Balboa, for the ruthless war hero, John Rambo, and kept evolving throughout his cinematic career.

He also wanted to go to Mirror Lake *to mourn* the recent death of his wife of forty years, if you could call it that. Sadly, most of his married life was void of happiness, love, children, and fulfillment. And now, he was finding it difficult to muster up any fond memories of his wife.

Adam Tiller and Marie Alston were high school sweethearts. They met at South Philadelphia High School, and both were the only child of blue collar working parents. They married at the age of twenty-three after graduating from college. Adam was a gifted writer, and earned a degree in Journalism from Temple University. Marie had a savvy mind for business and mathematics, and graduated from LaSalle College, summa cum laude. She would later become the CEO of the Tiller Publishing House in New York City, amassing a handsome fortune of her own.

Unfortunately, as successful as they both were in their respective professions, their marriage was a disaster. They were more business associates than husband and wife. It wasn't long after they tied the knot that most of the love, romance, laughter, communication, and intimacy came to an end. Adam had no idea how they were married for such a long time. Perhaps the money they made, the long hours at work and frequent travels, had created a comfort zone that kept them together. As long as they were able to ring up the big bucks, they could tolerate living under the same roof as *Mr. and Mrs. Adam Tiller.*

Adam sat alone on the plush white leather sofa in his Manhattan high rise apartment hoping to feel some kind of sadness or emptiness; anything that would connect him to his humanity. But all he had were regrets. He thought about how he and his wife met, and the day that they were married. It seemed so long ago. As newly-weds, their young lives were full of hope and promise, yet he couldn't figure out what happened. He had learned the hard way, that money doesn't buy happiness, or any of the most important things in life. He'd have given away his entire fortune to have had a happy marriage.

After a couple of years living in a modest row house in South Philadelphia, the Tiller's moved into a small apartment in Queens, New York, after Adam had written two novels that brought him considerable fame and fortune. It wasn't too long before he wrote the first of his many best sellers. As time passed on and their bank accounts grew, they were able to afford more expensive living quarters. Now, they were living *high on the hog* in a pricey high rise overlooking Central Park. This is when he believed that his marriage had become one in name only.

Adam picked up one of his wife's travel magazines that sat atop a stack of other magazines that he'd probably never get to read. He paged through it without giving much thought, until he came to a section called *Sales and Rentals.* He spied an advertisement for a log cabin that sat alone on a lake somewhere in the northwoods of Wisconsin. It caught his attention, and had the potential to serve as the perfect getaway. He decided to call the proprietor, a Michael Lucci, to obtain additional information. After a brief conversation with him, Adam liked what he heard, and told Lucci that he was going to fly out to see the cabin for himself. Money would be no object, so Adam offered more than the asking price in order for the owner to hold the property, until Adam could meet up with him. Lucci offered to pick up the renowned author at the airport in Rhinelander; only a short drive from the cabin.

In a couple of days Adam Tiller was on his way. He flew out of LaGuardia Airport to the city of Green Bay where he picked up a connecting flight to Rhinelander. Lucci was there when he arrived, and they quickly set out for the cabin. As Lucci drove along Route 17, Adam was very impressed by the wooded terrain, the quiet, and the remoteness of the area. It was something that he wasn't accustomed to experiencing in the *Big Apple.* They passed an Indian reservation before coming to Dam Lake, a large body of water that had several finger lakes. One of the bodies of water was called Mirror Lake, and unknown to most people including the locals, who for the most part, were members of the surrounding Indian reservations that border Dam Lake.

Adam immediately fell in love with the lake and the log cabin. Lucci didn't have to hurl any sales pitch in his direction for the cabin sold itself. As a young boy, Adam had belonged to a Boy Scout troop that went on overnight camping trips every month in the wooded areas of Pennsylvania and New Jersey. Coming to Mirror Lake brought back the same excitement that he once felt on his boyhood camping trips. He had a good feeling this place was going to be better than whatever his doctor could have prescribed.

He signed a four month lease with Lucci, a man that Adam figured to be in his mid-seventies. Lucci promised that Adam would leave Mirror Lake a different man. It was a gross understatement; for here begins the remarkable story about a lonely and unfulfilled man, a rustic log cabin, and a most miraculous lake. A story unlike any that you have ever read, and one that is too fantastic to believe.

Adam returned to Manhattan, and for the next couple of days tied up a number of loose ends, especially with Vincent Peale, the new CEO of Tiller Publishing House. He never liked Peale who was a greedy, pompous blow-hard. Adam had a suspicion that he and his wife were having an extra-marital affair, yet he had become too apathetic to confront either of them about it.

Peale wasn't in favor of Adam going so far away for four months, but was satisfied when Adam promised a new novel that would be unlike any he had ever written before and a sure best seller. He didn't inform his editor of exactly where he was going with it, nor did he tell him that he was planning to deviate from the usual type of work that had brought Adam a huge fan base, and that had raked in big bucks for Peale, too. He knew that Peale wouldn't accept anything else than the usual. Why would he? The Tiller's had made him a wealthy man, so it was for the best, at least for now, to say nothing.

Lucci had agreed to bring groceries to the cabin each week, so Adam could totally isolate himself from the outside world. Lucci's son would be the actual one delivering the groceries, and would be available to make any repairs on the cabin when necessary. Adam would leave a grocery list under the door mat on Friday morning, and the delivery would be made early Sunday. Adam didn't want to be disturbed, so the groceries would be left on the porch. Lucci didn't mind going out of his way, nor did his son, for he was being paid handsomely for his service.

Adam requested every week; a fresh order of large earthworms called *night crawlers,* but gave strict orders that Lucci's son was to place the carton in a separate bag. Before he left the cabin, he also asked Lucci to purchase a fishing rod along with a number of accessories. Lucci agreed and told him that everything he needed for a day on the lake would be stored in the backyard shed.

Adam didn't think it was necessary to meet Lucci or his son on the day he arrived at the airport about three in the afternoon, so he took a taxi to the cabin. The taxi driver looked puzzled when Adam asked to be dropped off along Route 17 in the middle of nowhere; however, after receiving a hundred dollar tip, he never said a word. Adam knew where to stop when he saw a sign advertising a favorite liquor of his. An unmarked trail, a few feet from the sign would lead him to the cabin. Adam packed light, only taking a suitcase and carry-on. If he needed any further clothing, he'd add it to his weekly list. He enjoyed strolling down the one mile trail for it was part of the beauty of the place. He took his time, but still had to rest once along the way. He wasn't in the greatest physical shape as when he was a young man. He was now, a sixty-three year old man, and feeling a lot older.

As he approached the cabin, he wondered how it could have been built in the middle of such thick brush. He laughed to himself imagining that it was dropped from the sky by a UFO. He walked to the porch and placed his luggage on a small wooden table that was set next to an old rocking chair. He rested on it for a few minutes to catch his breath and to survey the new environs. He took a moment to imagine how different his life was going to be in the next four months. There would be no television, radio, newspaper, fan mail, or calls from Peale. He didn't care if his apartment or publishing house burnt to the ground. He was determined to have no contact with the outside world, and looking forward to the peace and quiet, the fishing, and writing his new novel.

Unknown to Adam Tiller, was a secret surrounding Mirror Lake that would gradually unfold in the days ahead. What he was to experience in this remote corner of the world would be totally unexpected and for which he could have never had prepared.

Chapter Two

A Self Tour

As Adam sat on the porch, he realized that he was sweating, and could use a cold drink. The trees blocked any direct sunlight, but he wasn't feeling the effects of the sun, as much as the one mile walk having to carry his luggage. He studied the immediate surroundings. The cabin didn't sit directly on the lake. There was a small channel of water that passed in front of the cabin, and flowed into the lake. The channel was about twenty feet wide, and traveled two hundred feet before it reached its mouth.

He noticed a twelve foot wooden row boat tied to a small dock that would become his only mode of transportation and daily companion. It was a far cry from the yacht he owned and moored at his three million dollar summer house in Fort Lauderdale, but would be ample for the light fishing that he had intended to be doing. Lucci told him that the lake was well-stocked with an assortment of good eating fish, and that he would not be disappointed.

There was a gravel path between the dock and the side door of the cabin. There were two wooden steps in front of the cabin that stood no more than fifteen feet from the channel. He couldn't see the lake very well due to the thick brush between it and the cabin, so he'd have to wait until he rowed onto the lake before he could enjoy its beauty.

Before he entered the cabin, he checked out what was around it. There was a sizable backyard that included two sheds, an outside shower, and a chord of cedar logs whose sweet bouquet had reached Adam before he walked into the backyard. There was a propane-fueled grill and a picnic table where he could enjoy an outdoor meal. He also saw a generator that provided power for the cabin. In one shed he found a washer, and next to the shed tied between two trees was a clothesline. Adam smiled for he hadn't hung out clothing to dry in fifty years! Inside the second shed were the fishing rod and the accessories for which he had asked. There was also an ax, rake, broom, and a few other things including two bags of gravel.

Adam was impressed by the sturdiness of the cabin and its overall appeal. There were three doors on the cabin; one in the front, another on the trail-side, and a third in the back. There were two windows on every side that provided ample light. The lakeside of the cabin had thick brush and was several feet from the lake. There was a narrow path that separated it from the wooded area, so it was possible to walk completely around the cabin.

His new lodging didn't have a great view, as did his Manhattan apartment or winter house in Florida, yet the northwoods of Wisconsin had a beauty of its own. It was the cabin's remoteness, connection to nature, as well as its peace and quiet that gave it a unique and relaxing ambiance. If it wasn't for the channel that flowed by the cabin, it would be totally surrounded by thick brush. There was a rich variety of trees, many of which were extremely tall, and an assortment of shrubs that were tall and short, broad and narrow. There was a wide array of plants yielding colorful wild flowers that the author had never seen before.

Adam would later discover an abundance of animal life found in the wooded area including: deer, raccoon, porcupine, beaver, and opossum. There were reported sightings of bear, fox, and other animals living in the thickest part of the woods, but he hoped never to run into any of them. The trees made a perfect home for many birds, and the lake had its own assortment of ducks, loons, and larger wading birds such as the swan.

After his brief tour of the area directly surrounding the cabin, Adam brought his luggage inside, and began to check out his new lodging. Upon entering the cabin, he walked into a large living room that was furnished with a sofa, recliner, coffee table, two tables with lamps, and a magnificent stone fireplace. Adjacent to the living room, were the kitchen and a small eating area. There were enough windows that provided natural light during the day, but only when the sun was directly overhead would the cabin be fully lighted. The trees that filtered the sun throughout the morning and afternoon hours made for a cool and comfortable summer day.

The kitchen was equipped with a double stainless steel sink, refrigerator, electric stove, and food pantry. There were two cabinets on either side of a large double window behind the sink that looked into the backyard. In one cabinet were pots, pans, and other cookware, while in the second; were dinner plates, bowls, glasses, and cups. Below the sink were two drawers that held cooking and eating utensils. When Adam opened the fridge and the pantry, he found all the groceries that he ordered for his first week at Mirror Lake.

The cabin lacked all the usual amenities of a modern kitchen. There was no microwave oven or coffee maker; however, there was a toaster. The one extra that was missing in his humble abode was a bar. Adam was a reformed alcoholic and hadn't had a drink in two years. There were times when the alcoholic beverage that he held in his hand was his only friend, but it had proven in the long run to be his worst enemy. Instead of finding companionship with his wife or friends, he'd find it in a dry martini. He had not only become a lonely, unhappy and bored millionaire, but had also become a drunk. A friend intervened and convinced Adam to attend *AA* meetings. For the time being, he was everything mentioned above, but at least he wasn't a drunk.

When he first sobered up, he missed drinking quite a bit, but as the days passed, he lost all desire to do most of anything including drinking. His drinking oddly, never affected his writing, and it was the only time that he remained dry and sober. One of his most successful writing endeavors of his long career was a best seller he penned after he sobered up. The thought of writing better books kept him from taking the first drink that would lead him down the wrong path again, and this time there would be no guarantee that he would come out of it in one piece.

He finally followed a short hallway that led to two bedrooms. One had a standard-sized bed; the other had twins. Each room was furnished with a dresser, a chest of drawers, and a table with a lamp. Very few pieces of art or appointments were hung on the walls of the bedrooms. Each room had two framed prints that depicted scenes from nature; particularly, those found in the northwoods of Wisconsin.

Adam chose to sleep in the room with the standard-sized bed. He tossed his luggage on the bed, and would unpack later. Returning to the living room, he felt a slight chill in the air, so decided to start a fire. As he looked into the fireplace, he noticed that wood was already set up in what he remembered to be called a *box* fire. It jolted a memory from his days as a Boy Scout, when he learned that there were three kinds of material necessary to build a fire: kindling, tinder, and fuel. Kindling was made up of things that were easily ignited such as: bark, cotton, dried leaves, and very thin twigs. Tinder consisted of thicker twigs and small pieces of wood. Fuel included thick tree branches and logs. There were a few cedar logs placed around the kindling and tinder that gave the firewood its box appearance.

He wondered how he was going to start the fire since he had no matches. He smiled when he thought about one of the requirements to attain the rank of a Second Class Scout. As a Tenderfoot, the lowest rank in Scouting, he had to start a fire using a flint and steel set. A scout struck a flint stone with a strip of metal. The friction created a hot spark that would be directed to the kindling. Once he mastered this part, he waited until a spark struck the material and ignited it. At first, the scout would see smoke, then the redness of the material starting to burn. He'd begin blowing on the ember in the hope of getting a flame. Once he was able to get a flame, he could start feeding it, until it grew into a blazing campfire.

Feeling as if he was a Boy Scout, Adam searched for a flint and steel set or anything that he could use to start the fire. After looking around in a few different places, he found a can of charcoal fluid and a box of wooden stick matches under the sink. It would be a lot easier using these materials than a flint and steel set, yet not as much fun! He had a healthy fire going in no time.

He returned to the porch again, to write a schedule for the rest of the day. Before he wrote much, he put the pen down having caught himself. *Here I go again*. Adam was tired of the daily routine, having to plan everything he had to do, and meeting deadlines. It was something that he was now able to escape. He ripped the paper into four pieces and promised that he would do less planning while in the wilderness, and more often than not, be led in whatever direction the wind seemed to be blowing.

Chapter Three

A Fresh Start

The only things that Adam brought along with him from the high tech society to which he belonged were his smart phone and laptop. The former was only to be used in case of an emergency and the latter for writing his novel. He wouldn't read any e-mails or use the Internet, unless it involved research for his book. Ah, his book! He had absolutely no idea what he was going to write. He was hoping that coming to Mirror Lake would ignite a spark and mushroom into a new best seller.

Shortly after graduating college, Adam·was hired by *The Bulletin*, an evening newspaper in Philadelphia. For the most part he was an investigative reporter, and primarily covered police and crime stories. It proved to be a rich background for the fictional accounts of detective Allan Spalding, who spent thirty years fighting the mob, thieves, rapists, serial killers, drug dealers, and dirty cops.

He was finished writing this kind of novel. In fact, the last book in his Spalding series had an uncertain ending.

The reader was left with the uncertainty, as to whether Allan was killed or had escaped with his life. It was the sort of ending that could either bury the protagonist, or set up his glorious resurrection from the dead. Adam was determined to keep him in the grave.

Still thirsty, he went back into the cabin and made a cold glass of iced tea. He gazed at the loon kitchen clock that told him it was five o'clock. Lucci boasted of the magnificent sunsets on the lake, so he planned to take the boat out later in the afternoon to see for himself. He was also getting hungry, so chose to have something quick to eat before heading to view the sunset. Both the fridge and the pantry were well-stocked with food, and it didn't take long to opt for a ham and cheese sandwich along with potato chips and pickle spears. Presently, he settled for instant iced tea, but planned to make a pitcher of *sun-brewed tea* that his mother always had on the table when he was a boy.

Adam sat at the table alone. It didn't bother him for he found himself in this position many times in his life. While he was somewhere isolated writing his books, his wife would be out somewhere spending his and her own money with friends, clients, and acquaintances. Although he was not the socialite, Marie was always the life of the party, and a very amiable hostess. None of her charm, wit, or vibrant personality ever rubbed off on him. He was satisfied being the introverted writer allowing his wife to be her out-going self. Despite their distance over the years, there were times that he did miss her, if only because he was lonely. If he could only turn back the hands of time and start anew. Things would be different and far less painful than now;

but it was too late. There was no turning back. There was no hope.

After finishing off his modest meal, he cleaned up and returned to the porch. The huge evergreen trees blocked most of the view around him. He had to look down the channel to see what little of the lake was visible. He slowly rocked in the chair with nothing particular on his mind. He took a deep breath and enjoyed the sweet smell of the pines, spruces, and a host of other evergreens. The closest he had come to a similar experience was when Marie would spray their artificial Christmas tree with some artificial scent. But, this was the *real* deal. He already liked the new sights, sounds, and smells of the wilderness. He was glad that he had come to Mirror Lake.

As sunset was approaching, Adam made his way to the dock, untied the boat from its mooring, and carefully climbed into it. He used an oar to push off the grassy incline that was edged with a number of gray stones. When he backed up enough into the channel, he took the other oar, and began to row gently along the channel toward the lake. He was dumbfounded by its size and beauty. The woodlands hid Mirror Lake well, and Adam wondered how many people had ever laid eyes on it. The entire lake was arrayed in the most spectacular gold. Everything looked dazzling; the trees, water, sky, boat, and Adam as well. As he rowed further into the body of water, he was entertained by fish that were jumping playfully in and out of the lake. Birds of every feather flew graciously in the sky. Loons and other diving birds were picking one fish after the other from the water, as if there was an endless supply. A family of loons hurriedly passed the boat looking as if they were late for some engagement, and were trying to make up for lost time.

By the time he reached the middle of the lake, the sky had changed from gold to a brilliant orange. He was tired now, so stopped rowing and took a deep breath. He looked around and marveled at the beauty of the place. When he looked into the lake, he realized why it was called *Mirror* Lake. The surface of the water reflected everything, making it impossible to see into it. He couldn't determine the type of fresh water that comprised the lake, nor could he tell if it was polluted. He wondered if it was cedar water, so he cupped his hand, put it into the lake, and took out a water sample. He held it close to his nose and took a good whiff. It didn't smell like cedar, so ruled it out.

He thought that the water was relatively warm for early spring. He strained his eyes looking into the water, but saw nothing more than his own reflection. He had truly become an old man. His face showed its many wrinkles brought about by the years of reckless living. He was sickened by the bags under his eyes that were earned by his excessive drinking.

Adam Tiller didn't like what he saw, yet the lake could only reflect the truth of what was on the outside of a broken man. He began to pound the image on the lake; nearly falling out of the boat. As the sky once again changed to breath-taking shades of red, all that was heard on the lake, were the cries of an unhappy and unfulfilled man. He had missed how life was meant to be lived, and from becoming the happy man that he could have been by choosing a different path. It was a very painful self-revelation. Tears rolled down his cheeks. He buried his face in his hands and began to sob. So much beauty surrounded him, yet all he could feel was the ugliness that dwelt within. He picked up the oars, placed them in their locks, and began to row back to shore. The brilliant hues of red were overcome by the dark blue that marked the beginning of the night sky. By the time he reached his destination, it was pitch black. Had he not been wise to switch on the porch light, he would never have been able to find the cabin.

In a way, the cabin stood like a lighthouse that directed a lost vessel through rocky waters to safety. He didn't know it at the time, but the cabin would become his *beacon of hope*. As he approached the channel, he saw smoke rising from the chimney, and could smell the luscious scent of burning cedar. He worked an oar to pull the boat onto the embankment, and when he exited the skiff, pulled it out of the water. Not having a calendar of tides, he attached the boat to the dock with a rope. He couldn't afford losing his only mode of transportation.

He sat on the porch for a few minutes having gained his composure. He held the mental image of the magnificent sunset. It made him think of his dear mother, a devout Catholic, who told him as a young boy, that when looking at such an example of natural beauty to always, "Remember the Artist." Adam thought that despite man's ingenuity, he could never duplicate the spectacle that he had just experienced.

His eyes once again began to fill, as he thought of his parents who always told him that he was their *miracle* baby.

His mother had given birth to him at forty-four. His dad was almost fifty. He wasn't a planned pregnancy, but both of his parents made it clear how much they loved him. Sadly, he felt cheated as a boy, for his parents were already in their fifties when he was old enough to understand things. He longed to have had a more youthful mom and dad, who could play ball with him, and do the things that the younger parents of his friends would do.

Neither of his parents would live to see him graduate college, land his first job, or get married. They weren't there when he made his first million, yet this would not have impressed them very much. They were simple, modest, and hard working. They were able to set their priorities straight early in their married life and savored every minute of the time that they spent together. God came first, their marriage second, and Adam third. Amassing material possessions wasn't a goal, nor was keeping up with the Jones.' They were the type of people who made friends easily, kept the good ones forever, and were respected by everyone. If only Adam had emulated their way of life, perhaps he would be a happier man. He spent his entire life attaining everything he wanted, yet had gained nothing that he truly needed.

As he rose from the rocking chair, he peered at what little of the sky he saw overhead. It was filled with stars, constellations, and the moon shining brilliantly over the lake. He should have stayed longer on the lake. He was certain that it would have had a different, yet equally enjoyable appeal. There were more evenings still to come on Mirror Lake, so he knew that he could take pleasure in the night sky at a future date. He had taken in more than enough on his first day in the wilderness. He was now exhausted, both physically and emotionally. It was time to call it a day.

He noticed that with nightfall came different sounds. Instead of entering the cabin, he chose to sit down a short while longer; listening to the lake and its surroundings speak to him. The sounds of cheerful birds were replaced by the sounds of bullfrogs croaking and plucking their strings to a tune that Adam had never before heard. He was astounded by how well-orchestrated their music was being played. He continued to hear the splashing of fish in the water, but the insect world was gradually taking over; being dominated by the joyful chirping of crickets. He heard the hooting of an owl, and the scurrying of some animal in the woods across from him.

A slow moving mist approached from the lake along with a sudden chill. He rose from the chair once again, but this time made his way into the cabin. He stirred the embers in the fireplace, and added a couple of cedar logs to the fire. He made a cup of hot chocolate that he topped with mini-marshmallows. He laughed as he thought of what he would normally be drinking at this time of the night when he was alone. He sat on the sofa near the fireplace, and wrapped himself in a soft crocheted Afghan throw; weaved with strains of earthen colors that appropriately matched the rustic world into which he had suddenly been immersed.

Adam could hardly believe where he was or what he was doing. Despite how he felt when the lake had revealed the worse of him, he was starting to feel an inner peace.

Oh, what a good cry could do for the soul! Little did he realize that Mirror Lake was having a positive effect on him. After taking a sip of his beverage, he looked wearily into the fire, watching the flames shift from one color to the next and dance from one log to another. Although it wasn't his intention, Adam would be spending the first night at Mirror Lake sleeping on the sofa, and not having to worry about soiling his freshly-made bed.

Chapter Four

A Man in Flux

The alarm on Adam's wrist watch sounded at four thirty a.m. He had set it the night before, so he wouldn't miss the rising of the sun. He looked into the fireplace, and saw a few embers amidst ashes gasping to stay alive. He stirred them up, and added a couple more logs hoping that the dying embers were hot enough to restart the fire. He was successful. Knowing that he wasn't planning to stay very long on the lake, he added a couple more logs, so the cabin would be warm and cozy upon his return.

He took out a can of Folgers coffee and had to read the directions on the back of the can, for he hadn't used a stove and pot to brew coffee since the sixties. After he added a few scoops of coffee and water into the pot, he turned on the stove hoping that it would work. He breathed a sigh of relief when the coil on the electric stove reddened. He placed the coffee pot on the coil, and wondered what he was going to have for breakfast.

He took out a box of Wheaties from the pantry, and poured some into a large bowl. He sliced a banana, and added it along with milk and a little sugar. Forgetting for a moment where he was, he looked on the table for the morning newspaper. He sat at the table, and was mesmerized by the sight and sound of the coffee starting to percolate. The aroma of the freshly-brewed *mountain grown* coffee filled the shanty, and made his mouth water with delight. After he poured himself a mug and sipped it, he concluded that it was the best coffee that he had tasted in years. He filled a thermos with the coffee, and planned to take it with him to the lake. He chose to pack a few munchies in the event that he'd be on the lake longer than he anticipated. The loon kitchen clock reminded him that it would soon be time to leave, so he quickly unpacked and changed into his sweat suit. He grabbed his light collation, and headed for the boat.

There was a slight mist coming off the water as he rowed down the channel toward the lake. He wondered if it was there all night or if it had just moved in. He had timed the sunrise perfectly. Just as he arrived at the main body of the lake, light started to replace the darkness. The sun gradually ascended from the horizon, thus creating the dawn of another day. The sky was a canvas of brilliant and changing colors; one more sublime than the other. It was a phenomenal sight to behold.

Adam took his time rowing the bark taking long deliberate strokes, so that his heart rate would gradually climb. When he approached what seemed to be the middle of the lake, he pulled the oars from their locks, and sat relishing this spectacle of nature. *Man could do a lot of things, but never could he duplicate the wonders created by the Divine Architect.* He started a debate with himself over what event was the most spectacular—the sun's rising or its setting. In the end, he called it a draw for both were equally plush and breath-taking.

The mist covered the entire lake, and Adam could see no water beneath the vessel. He opened the thermos and took a sip of coffee. He thought of what it would be like fishing, but since he hadn't taken his rod and tackle box, had to settle with finding out later in the day. There was plenty of time for fishing, so for now, he was content with taking in the majesty of his first morning on Mirror Lake. Sitting on a lake in the middle of nowhere, and having nothing to do, was a far cry from what Adam was accustomed to doing in the hustle and bustle of life in the big city. There was no doubt in his mind where he'd rather be. He wondered why he hadn't thought of doing this for himself years ago. Maybe he'd be happier, and life would seem to be worth living.

For the next hour Adam reminisced about a lot of things. He thought of Marie. She would have liked this place. Too bad she wasn't here to enjoy his newly-found paradise. For a short time, he thought about writing his book, but didn't come up with any acceptable ideas. He opened the satchel, and took out a green apple to nibble on. After one last sip of coffee, he began his return trip to the cabin. As the boat drifted along the water, it seemed as if it was moving across a dense cloud more than a lake. It brought to mind a classical scene from the hit musical, *The Phantom of the Opera* that he and his wife had seen three times on Broadway. He envisioned the demented phantom steering his craft, a large sea shell, through a similar mist to his secret labyrinth.

Upon arriving at his hovel, Adam sat on the porch and watched as the mist finally dissipated. His nose picked up the freshness in the air, and his ears heard the arcane sounds of the animal world awaking from its slumber. The more time Adam spent in the wilderness, the more acute his five senses would become. All the noise and distractions of the big city had dulled his senses, but the new surroundings were having a honing effect on them. At Mirror Lake he would return to a simpler, yet invigorating life. It would bring him closer to nature, and to the soul that lived within the shell named, Adam Tiller. He would rediscover the God he knew and loved in his youth, but had forgotten throughout most of his adult life. Once he had established a successful career, he didn't need God anymore. At Mirror Lake he'd reconnect with God, and in doing so, would discover his true self.

The cabin had held its warmth well, yet Adam added a couple more logs to maintain the heat, until the full sun could provide it naturally. It was a good time to finish his unpacking. As he put away the remainder of the things he brought along, he thought of all the suitcases and bags that Marie took with her on a typical vacation. He had forgotten how to travel light and liked it.

He set up his toiletries in the bathroom that was situated between the two bedrooms. There was a bath tub, but oddly no shower. Marie loved to take a bath and would pamper herself for hours sitting in water that was treated with Calgon bath oil beads. Adam, on the other hand preferred to take quick showers. He didn't like the idea of bathing in dirty water. He remembered noticing the outdoor shower last night, so it was where he'd be taking his daily shower. After unpacking, he made his way to the shower, and even though it had only cold water, found it to be quite refreshing. He returned to the cabin and put on a clean sweat suit. He poured another mug of coffee, and nestled on the recliner to enjoy the warmth of the fireplace.

His eyes traveled across the living room studying its contents. Above the fireplace, as often seen in log cabins, was the head of a buck with a full set of antlers. Lucci told him, when giving a tour of the property, that it was killed by his son in the surrounding woods. In one corner of the room was the largest stuffed raccoon perched on a limb that Adam had ever seen. It looked as if it could jump off the bark and scoot right out the front door. In another corner of the room stood a large six foot black bear. It wasn't hunted by Lucci's son, but was representative of the bears that dwell in some areas of the northwoods. Adam smiled to himself when he thought that Marie would never have liked the woodsy motif of the living room. Her indoor domain would be the bath tub and fireplace, and no more!

Adam looked around expecting to see a shot gun mounted on the wall. Fear swept through his mind as he imagined coming face to face with a ferocious bear, and not having anything with which to defend himself. He calmed down, as he recalled Lucci telling him that none had ever been sighted in the wooded area surrounding Mirror Lake. He did add, however, that it was more likely coming into contact with deer, coons and possums, porcupines, and an occasional fox. *Nope, Marie wouldn't like this place after all, despite the gorgeous sunrise and sunset. She'd never get passed the spiders and other annoying insects, let alone any animal that might cross her path!* Although he wasn't necessarily afraid of what was "out" there, he still opted to secure all the doors and windows each evening before retiring; just to play safe.

There was one more item located in the living room that brought Adam the most interest. He rose from the recliner, and walked over to study it more closely. It was a bookcase stuffed with several volumes of classics, mostly about the outdoors. He spied an old book written by Jack London called *White Fang* that Adam read in the fifth grade. There were books about Indians, pioneers, hunters, and naturalists. He saw *The Last of the Mohicans* by James Fenimore Cooper that he read in high school. He picked up a book, rather a tome that he began reading in college, but never had the time or patience to finish. It was the classic saga of the strong-willed Captain Ahab, and his quest for the great white whale *Moby Dick* written by Herman Melville.

He took the novel with him as he returned to the recliner, closed his eyes, and thought of the movie version of the book starring Gregory Peck, who portrayed the obsessed sea captain. It was much easier having seen the movie than to have read the book, but the beauty of a book is the imagination the reader uses in the experience. In a movie, very little is left to the imagination. It is the reason Adam loved being a writer.

He decided to give it another shot. He brought the book to the bedroom, and placed it on the night stand. He chose to read it at least a half hour each night in bed. He also planned to take a daily walk in the woods, go fishing late afternoon or early evening, and to write before retiring. If all of his daily routine didn't tire him out by the end of the day, surely reading *Moby Dick* would do the trick. As it would turn out to be, Adam Tiller would read the book in its entirety, as well as several others. He would reread books that he already read, or started decades ago. He would find new meaning in them, and be able to find much more enjoyment. Yes, Adam was indeed, a man in flux.

Chapter Five

A Walk in the Woods

Adam heated a can of Campbell's chicken noodle soup for lunch, once again using the stove top. Normally, he'd use a microwave, but he had chosen to live a more pristine life at least for a few months. He boiled a pot of water, and tossed a couple of Nathan's hot dogs into it. In a smaller pot he warmed sauerkraut, his favorite topping for franks. He couldn't recall the last time he made lunch for himself. It was either a meal to skip or to be eaten at a restaurant, café, or deli in Manhattan. When he was writing, he feasted on his favorite culinary vice—fast foods.

The smell of the boiling franks reminded him of going to the ballpark to watch a Phillies baseball game. Even though he lived in New York, a rival town, he still held the allegiance to the boys in the red pinstripes. He was a season ticket holder for years, and had attended every home game in the 1980 and 2008 World Series Championship years. He gave up his season tickets a couple of years ago, but was present for every game played against the Mets and

Yankees in New York. This would be the first summer that he wouldn't see a game, unless his team made the play-offs and the World Series.

Marie never liked baseball, and wasn't as loyal to "The City of Brotherly Love," as was her husband. She was quick to adapt to living in New York. On the other hand Adam was a Philadelphian at heart; even though he lived in a plush Manhattan high rise, and worked in the city for years. He never lost his taste for soft pretzels, cream cheese, Philly cheese steaks, or his love for all Philly sports teams. An old bowling buddy once said it best when he exclaimed, "You can take the boy out of Philly, but you can't take Philly out of the boy!"

Among his favorite memories of the Phillies were the games he attended with his dad as a young boy. It didn't matter what team won the game. What did matter the most was that Adam went to the game with his father. He and his dad would take a bus from their modest row house in South Philly to Center City, and hop on the Broad Street Subway to Lehigh Avenue. They'd walk several city blocks to Shibe Park that later was renamed Connie Mack Stadium in honor of the former manager of the Phils, who holds the record for most victories in baseball history. He never complained about the walk up Lehigh Avenue because along the route stood street merchants selling baseball caps, pennants, baseballs, and all sorts of nifty souvenirs. When it came to going to a Phillies game with his son, Mister Tiller couldn't turn down the opportunity. He was never too busy, nor did he ever have to work late. Adam really missed him.

1964 wasn't a very good year for his dad, or the Phillies. It started out great for the home team. Jim Bunning hurled a perfect game on Father's Day, and the Phils were well ahead in the pennant race late into the season. He remembered when he and his dad welcomed the team as they arrived at Philadelphia International Airport. There were only ten games left in the season, and all they had to do was to win just one to secure the pennant. He sung a few bars of a song that was written by pitcher, Dennis Bennett. It was about going to the doctor for a shot because the team had "pennant fever." He had never forgotten the words, or how the great season of hope had ended.

The Phillies lost every one of their remaining ten games, and the Saint Louis Cardinals snuck in to win the pennant. He recalled how he and his dad cried as the season came to an abrupt end. It was very disappointing for the Tiller's and the entire city. However, Adam would be crying for something much worse a couple of months later, namely, the sudden death of his beloved father. His dad would never experience the glory years, when the team led by Mike Schmidt, Larry Bowa, and Steve Carlton won three straight National League titles. He would miss the 1980 season with the addition of long-time Cincinnati Red player, Pete Rose that would finally bring the coveted baseball prize, the World Series, to the city of Philadelphia.

His father would also have liked the 2008 team that starred Ryan Howard, Chase Utley, Cole Hammels, and Brad Lidge. They were instrumental in bringing the world championship trophy back to Philly. Although he wasn't alive to watch the two World Series championships on earth, Adam always thought that God had provided his dad with a box seat in heaven's grandstand!

After enjoying lunch and reminiscing about his dad and Phillies' baseball, he elected to take a walk in the woods. One of the things that he didn't want to do was to get lost, so he chose not to venture too far from the cabin. In addition to the small trail that connected the dirt road where he was left off by the taxi, there was another trail he noticed. This was the one that he'd take today.

Since the light of the sun was blocked by the many trees, the temperature was considerably cooler along the trail than on the lake, so he chose to wear a sweat suit. At the outset of his hike, he looked for a tree limb, long and narrow enough to be used as a walking stick. He hadn't strolled more than a hundred yards from the cabin, when he found one that was perfect. Using a skill that he learned as a scout, he set landmarks along the trail; just in case he would get lost. He also observed that every so often, he'd come upon a tree had a red mark on it. He supposed that Lucci or his son painted them on trees in the event that someone would get lost. He was determined that he wasn't going to be the first person to be placed on the list. He thought of returning to the cabin for his cell phone, but decided to rough it. He found pleasure in being more attentive to his surroundings and playing the old Boy Scout.

Walking through the woods ended up being an enjoyable and invigorating endeavor. It was a far cry from what he was used to seeing in what movie director John Huston called *The Asphalt Jungle.* He entertained himself by trying to identify the trees, bushes, wild flowers, and other flora. At times he took a leaf or flower of a plant he couldn't identify, and would later go to the Internet in the hope of finding out what it was. He smiled, when he saw a particular plant that the *Boy Scout Handbook* warned to avoid by the catchy phrase of "Leaflets three, let it be." Poison Ivy was the very first poisonous plant that he learned to identify after having taken home a bad case of it from his very first camping trip! He itched and itched for days.

He also came upon another familiar, yet friendlier plant that had a very recognizable leaf shape. He pulled out a sprig of *sassafras* from the ground, and chewed on its root. He recalled making sassafras tea by boiling its roots in water, while once on a survival camping trip; one of the requirements that he had to meet in attaining the rank of Star Scout. For a brief moment he thought of pulling out a few more sprigs to take back to the cabin, but nixed the idea knowing that he'd prefer sun-brewed Lipton iced tea.

As he walked further along the trail, he spied something scurrying behind a holly bush about twenty feet ahead. He squatted and waited patiently for the little critter to make the next move. It didn't take very long for the animal to identify itself. It was a porcupine. He hadn't ever seen one outside of the zoo, and didn't want to get any closer in fear of being stung by its quills. It wobbled slowly away from him, and made its way deeper into the woods. When he thought that he was at a safe distance, Adam rose from the ground, and continued along the trail.

Very little sunlight penetrated the canopy, but when a ray of light did find its way through an opening, it produced a dazzling effect. As if it was meant for his enjoyment, a beam of light caught dust particles, and struck a tree stump with a radiant splash. It signaled a perfect place to rest. Adam sat on the stump, and took a couple deep breaths. He was perspiring heavily, so from his hooded sweatshirt pulled out a cold bottle of water. It was extremely quiet in the woods. Adam was amazed that as he was sitting on the tree stump, he could actually hear his heart beating.

Being alone in the woods triggered a memory when he, and his best friend, while on a hike with the Boy Scout troop, argued whether or not a falling tree made noise, if no one was present to hear it. He still couldn't come up with a definitive answer fifty years later. He followed a line of tall trees that were moving as wind was making its way toward him. The sound of their rustling leaves brought pleasure to his ears. He closed his eyes, and allowed the cool refreshing breeze to travel across his sweaty face. Goose bumps tingled up his spine as the feeling of the wind against his face and the sound of the rustling leaves, brought him to a euphoria achieved by hikers, joggers, and mountain climbers. At one point, he thought he heard a whispering sound traveling along the row of trees. For all he knew, it could have been God trying to communicate to him by using the wonderful medium of created nature. Adam thought that even an atheist, when walking through the woods and having a similar experience, had to consider the proof of God's existence based on His created effects. He was enjoying the *present moment* so much that he didn't want to get up and move on.

Looking in another direction he noticed a large tree that had fallen. He stood up, and decided to get a closer look. He assumed that it was struck by lightning a long time ago because it exhibited a vast amount of decay. He saw an army of termites marching back and forth across the shaft of the tree. He hoped that none had been on the tree stump where he had just rested. He started to scratch himself, as if there were termites walking all over him. *Isn't it funny how one's imagination can bring on such physical symptoms.* As he was looking upward, he spied a number of nests perched atop several tall trees. As he wondered whether they were bird nests or nests of other animals; it made him forget about the termites.

Adam felt that he had ventured far enough from the cabin, so it was time to make his way back. He thought that he had put in a good hour along the trail, and there was another hour of walking still ahead of him. On the way back he noticed that the chatter of birds had intensified. Perhaps it was because he more aware of what was around him. A sudden feeling emerged from deep inside of him. He had allowed so much of his life pass by without having been attentive to it. He was saddened to think that there was so much of life that he had missed. If only he had seen and appreciated the tree, rather than trying to capture the entire forest. If he had only stopped to smell the roses, feel the soft raindrops against his face, or watch a dazzling sunset. Enjoying life's simple pleasures would have made his life worth living.

He stooped down occasionally to overturn a rock or tree limb in the hope of finding some creature living under it. It was something that he had learned to do in the Boy

Scouts, while at summer camp one year. He once found a red eft under a rock, and took it back with him to the cabin. It became his special pet for the remainder of the week. Another time, he discovered a ribbon snake under an old decayed log, but hoped that he wouldn't find one this time around for he had lost his taste for exotic pets over the years. It didn't seem that it took very long to be back at the cabin. *Funny how all trips home, seem to take less time.* He had been gone for over two hours, and the walk certainly had worked up an appetite. It is an effect that the wilderness always has on people . . . and how tastier food seems to be when eaten outdoors!

When Adam was about fifty feet from his abode, he saw a fawn nibbling on the bark of a tree. It was beautiful, and still having its white spots on a seemingly very soft pelt. He fell to his knees, so not to spook it. Suddenly, two other deer approached, and began to have their way with the bark as well. There was a buck with a full rack of antlers, and its mate. Adam had never before seen a family of deer, and was enjoying every minute of it. As the fawn moved away from the tree, the doe quickly followed behind it, so it would not venture too far from it. After observing the deer for five minutes Adam stood up, and as he took a couple of steps toward them, they immediately darted deeper into the woods.

Adam brought a few cedar logs into the cabin, and set them next to the fireplace for later in the evening. He took a quick shower, and changed into his last sweat suit. He was already thinking of washing some clothes. As summer advanced, he thought that he'd need more clothing, so would eventually add a few pieces of apparel to the list for

Lucci's son. He forgot about making sun-brewed tea, so settled for instant. He poured himself a glass, picked up a bag of pretzels, and made his way to the porch. Albeit it was a delightful walk through the woods, the exercise tired him out, and he was starting to feel a bit achy. Not only were his five senses being sharpened, but so were the muscles in his body that hadn't been used in years, being stretched. He knew that exercise was good for both his body and mind, so he promised himself that he would continue walking every day. Little did he realize how much it would also do for his soul?

Hanging from one of the posts that supported the roof of the porch was a wooden plaque of a big mouth bass that had a thermometer attached to it. It was seventy degrees, and part of the picture perfect first day that Adam was having. He looked down the channel to the lake and spotted a large fish jump out and back into the water, as if it was luring him to jump into the boat saying, *Catch me, if you can!* If Adam wasn't so hungry, he'd have taken the bait; however, once he filled his belly, he was determined to give it a try. He wasn't a fisherman, but had read in some magazine that the best time to catch fish, especially the big mouth bass, was in the late afternoon and early evening. He checked the metal bait box on the other end of the porch, and found a white cardboard pint-sized container filled with soil and a dozen night crawlers ready to lure a few fish of their own.

Looking into the channel, he noticed a loon that was very busy swimming back and forth, and occasionally would jump out of the water to make its way to a birch tree that hardly had any leaves on it. It was making that same eerie sound that he had heard a number of times on the boat. He had found finally its source. Upon closer inspection, Adam saw what seemed to be a nest perched at the base of the trunk. He waited until the loon returned to the channel, then proceeded toward the tree. His suspicion was confirmed for it was a bird's nest, but the biggest surprise was that there was another loon resting on it. He slowly backed off, and returned to the porch. Within a minute or two, the male loon jumped out of the water and waddled to the nest. He seemed like the expectant father pacing up and down the waiting room, a nervous wreck! He smiled and closed his eyes wondering what it may have been like having shared the same experience, or better, what it may have been like to have children of his own?

Looking at the scene under the tree, he envisioned what it would be like having a family of loons living near the cabin. The thought intrigued him, and brought him a feeling of joyful anticipation. It had been a long time since Adam Tiller felt as excited about something, relaxed, and at peace. His first twenty-four hours at Mirror Lake were simply amazing; however, the best was still yet to come.

Chapter Six

Casting Away

After eating a tuna sandwich, potato chips, and a pickle, Adam was ready for a nap. He stretched out on the sofa, and fell asleep within a few minutes. The fresh air of the outdoors seemed to have knocked him out. He awakened at three o'clock, and gathered all he needed for his fishing adventure. He pushed off the embankment, and headed for the lake. He opted to stay close to the cabin, and then gradually make his way along the land searching for trees whose branches were extended over the water. This created shady spots, a favorite resting place for big mouth bass. Once he found a shady spot, he dropped anchor, and began to prepare his rod. It was a light Zebco push-button kind that was easy to cast; unlike the spinner-type that took some practice to master. He opened the tackle box that contained a variety of artificial lures including spoons, plugs, spinners, and plastic worms in a variety of colors sporting small propellers, and straight or curly tails. He also took the carton of night crawlers in the event that the fish preferred to *taste* their food rather than to just swallow it.

It had been several years since he did any serious freshwater fishing, but he remembered some strategies including the choice of lures. He chose a red and white striped spoon known commonly as a "Daredevil." He tied a small metal swivel to the end of the line that would make it easier to switch lures, and then he attached the spoon. He stood in the boat, held the rod over his head, and then let loose . . . *Let the games begin!*

He was very impressed with himself as the first cast flew high through the air, and landed about forty feet from the boat. He waited a few seconds for the spoon to sink deeper into the lake, and then slowly began to reel in the line. He felt a wiggling motion made by the spoon as it moved against the water. It seemed that the lure was dancing as it made its way back to the skiff. Its movement, noise, and glitter made by its silver underbelly, caught a beam of sunlight that made it extremely enticing to a hungry fish. As the spoon reached the halfway point between the boat, and where it had been cast, Adam felt a hit.

He gave the rod a quick jerk to assure that the fish was hooked, and not just nibbling around the treble hook. Once again, the mirror effect of the lake prevented him from looking into the water to see what was on the end of the line. When the catch was only a couple of feet from the boat, he reached for a short-handled net in the event that the fish would snap its way off the hook. He placed the net under the fish while still in the water, and just as it became visible, scooped it out of the water. His first trophy was a beautiful yellow perch that had to be close to a foot long.

The fisherman used a small set of pliers designed to unhook fish, and carefully removed the spoon from its mouth without hurting it. He gently returned the perch to the water. Adam puffed with pride having caught a fish on his very first attempt. As the next couple of hours passed, there were many more fish that he took aboard. Without having to change the spoon, he hooked three more yellow perch, two crappies, and a pickerel that had to have been almost two feet long, four small bass, and an eel that gave him a heap of trouble while extracting the hook. The creature wrapped itself around the line, so all Adam could do was to cut the line; not wanting to bring it aboard the boat.

The only fish that had escaped him was the big mouth bass; the one fish that he wanted to hook the most. Knowing its taste for live worms, and that it liked to hang out in shady spots, Adam made his way to an ideal place closer to the shore. He found a tree that was sprawled over the lake, and switched from the spoon to a night crawler that had to measure six inches in length. He made sure that the snelled hook he attached to the swivel passed through a healthy portion of the worm, so it wouldn't be torn off by a mere nibble. He stood in the boat, and cast the line perfectly to the other side of the shade. He waited a couple of seconds, and then began to slowly reel in the line. It didn't seem that it moved a foot when he felt a major strike. He jerked the rod, and began to reel in the line with greater speed. The fish gave him a tremendous fight out-performing the one given him by the pickerel. Suddenly, the fish jumped out of the water to reveal itself as a huge big mouth bass. When the fish splashed back into the lake, it felt as if it had escaped. Adam's heart drop, but as he continued to reel in the line, he could once again feel the tug of the bass. He hadn't had this much excitement in years!

He finally had the fish close enough to the vessel to net it. *What a beauty!* It was the largest big mouth bass that he had ever seen, and a certain trophy winner had he been in some sort of angling competition. Too bad that no one was around to see it, or that his cell phone was in the cabin. He could have at least taken a photo to prove that he wasn't making up any *fish tales*. Without any evidence of the catch, it would be a difficult story for anyone at home to believe. Sadly, he unhooked the bass without hurting it, and returned it to the lake.

Adam's first fishing adventure was capped by another remarkable sunset. How quickly the hours passed on the lake. It was only the first of many more fishing days ahead, and this made Adam very happy. He hoped that it wasn't just beginner's luck today. His concern would be allayed the next time he'd go out . . . and the next . . . and the next. Lucci wasn't fibbing. Mirror Lake was indeed, lavishly stocked.

He remained on the lake until the sky had finished its color show, and now was eager to enjoy what the nightfall canvas would provide. He wasn't disappointed for the sky was clear, and displayed a vast number of stars. He was able to easily identify half dozen constellations, as well as the planets Mars and Jupiter. A full moon was perched brilliantly in the sky, and illuminated the lake and its surroundings. He felt as if the celestial body was smiling at him. The same feeling of euphoria that he experienced in the woods returned, and almost lifted him out of the boat. The sky was now, as black as obsidian, yet he could still see the entire cabin unlike last night when he only saw its light. He pulled up the wooden oars, and began to row back safely with the light of the moon guiding his every stroke.

As he approached the lodge, he eyed a large raccoon helping itself to a bowl of pretzels that he left on the porch. He should have known better than to leave food where animals could easily have access to it. His mistake, however, provided some unexpected entertainment. The critter wasn't eating out of the bowl, as would a dog or a cat. Instead, it stood on its hind legs holding each pretzel in its small paws; making it appear quite human. It stared at the intruder as if to say, "Come on, I dare you to take it from me!" Adam didn't move a muscle and continued to watch the masked-bandit finish off his snack. He finally spoke to his guest saying, "Would you like to come inside for a cold beer, my friend?" As he started to laugh aloud, the coon decided that it was time to depart, so dropped to all fours and nonchalantly made its way from the porch to the back of the cabin. Adam watched with glee as his uninvited guest disappeared into the darkness. *And he didn't even leave me a tip!*

Just as last night, by this time Adam was exhausted and hungry. He was surprised to discover that he had acquired a slight bit of sunburn, even though he was in the sun for only a short period of time. He was glad that he didn't start off early in the morning for he'd be as red as a lobster. He rinsed off the fishing rod and other accessories with a hose on the side of the cabin, and returned them to the shed in the backyard. Even though the moon provided light around the cabin, he still flicked on the light switch of the shower stall knowing that he'd be taking a late night shower. He fetched all the things needed to wash up, and after another cold yet refreshing shower, headed back to the cabin for something to eat.

It was time for his first real meal at Mirror Lake, so he chose to go all out. He started by preparing a salad. He cut up half a head of Romaine lettuce, and placed it in a large bowl. He took a variety of vegetables from the fridge, and began to slice, cut, or dice a cucumber, tomato, red onion, and a large mushroom. He shredded a carrot and a piece of cheddar cheese. He added all the veggies to the bowl, stirred it, and placed it in the fridge. He would later douse the salad with a creamy Italian dressing, and top it off with seasoned croutons and bacon bits.

He boiled half a stainless steel pot of water on the stove, tossed in a pinch of salt, and added a half pound of rigatoni pasta. He cooked it for only seven minutes to assure that it would be "ad dente," strained it, and poured it into another bowl. He took the tomato sauce that he heated, and issued it over the pasta. He removed a half loaf of garlic bread that he had plopped into the oven. He placed the food on the kitchen table and set out a plate, small bowl, cup, and eating utensils. In a few minutes he'd be enjoying an "Italian Night" at Mirror Lake. The only things missing were a bottle of merlot wine and a Verdi opera providing a relaxing background. After pouring a glass of iced tea, he sat at the table, and for the first time in ages was missing Marie.

Iced tea would have to do for tonight. He could have easily ordered a few bottles of wine, but he was sticking to the promise he made that he was no longer going to drink or smoke. He was determined to make the sun-brewed tea early tomorrow morning, and would later write a note to remind himself to make it. He enjoyed his meal very much, and suspected that it was an effect of being on the lake for a few hours. His mother would be proud of the dinner that he had whipped up, and the home-made ice tea would be icing on the cake the next time. Even though his sauce was store bought, it didn't seem all that bad. He recalled Marie's attempt to make sauce from scratch. It would never come close to that of his mother's *gravy*, as she'd called it, being Italian. Of course he'd never admit it to his wife. Maybe he'd try making his own gravy from scratch while at Mirror Lake. He supposed that he should also remind himself of this, too. In the last few months Adam had difficulty remembering things. He feared that it was an early sign of Alzheimer's disease although he never spoke to his doctor about it. He wasn't looking forward to old age, its aches and pains, disease, and inevitably death. He quickly dismissed anymore ill—thoughts; not wanting to spoil his enjoyable dinner.

It was very different, if not eerie, eating such a fine dinner alone. He was used to the background chatter of people eating in the many eateries he frequented throughout his life, or at least he had Marie with whom to chat. He was uncomfortable with the deafening silence, yet in time he would grow accustomed to it. Despite having to dine with himself, he did enjoy dinner. After he washed the pots and pans, dinnerware, and utensils without the use of a dishwasher, he restarted the fire. Before plopping on the recliner to relax he stood in front of the bookcase looking for something to read.

His eyes widened with delight when he saw one of his favorite boyhood classics written by Daniel Defoe—*Robinson Crusoe*. He picked it up, turned on the floor lamp and slumped down into the recliner. In a way he felt like his childhood hero who was shipwrecked, and had to weather the many storms associated with surviving on a deserted island. At least he didn't have to deal with any cannibals! Adam tried to recall some of his memorable parts of the book such as Crusoe's discovery of the human footprint that led him to conclude that he wasn't alone on the island.

His favorite part by far was the discovery of a man, a *good* cannibal, who Crusoe named "Friday." There was a great friendship that developed between them; one that he had envied. Adam never enjoyed a friendship like it as a boy, or as an adult. He would have given half his fortune in exchange for a true friend. He thought at one time that his wife would become his best friend, but it never happened. He recounted the great disappointment he felt when the castaway finally left his island paradise, and wondered if he'd feel the same when it was time to depart from Mirror Lake.

Although he planned to read *Moby Dick* every night in bed, he would have to put it off for now. He poured himself another glass of iced tea before sitting on the recliner to read. He spread the Afghan blanket across his legs, and entered into a different kind of wilderness. Before he knew it, Adam finished reading the classic from cover to cover. He added two more logs to the fire, and gazed at the dancing flames as he reflected on something that he had not gleaned from the book when he read it over a half century ago, namely, Crusoe's awareness of Divine Providence in his life. Once again, he had connected with his boyhood hero, and just as Crusoe grew closer to his Creator on a secluded island, so would Adam in the wilderness of northern Wisconsin. For the first time in years, Adam Tiller began to pray.

Chapter Seven

An Astonishing Catch

*O*ur modern hero didn't plan to rise from bed early in the morning. He hadn't experienced as much physical activity in the last decade as he had in the last couple of days, so he elected to sleep in. When he finally did awaken, he was surprised at how well the cabin had held its warmth. There weren't more than a few embers still alive in the fireplace, so he opted to let the fire burn out itself. The loon clock showed that it was nine o'clock.

Having feasted last night, Adam settled for a light breakfast that consisted of a toasted bagel with butter, a ripe banana, and a cup of coffee. As he was preparing a fresh pot of coffee, he found himself whistling. It was something that he had forgotten how to do. As he ate his meal, he fiddled with the idea of taking out his laptop to start writing his new book, but he hadn't given it much thought. Usually, he'd pen a brief summary plot, outline, and a minor description of his main characters.

In earnest, Adam didn't want to write. He'd much rather go fishing. He liked the thought of a healthy tan, and was curious about what other fish might be found in the center of the lake and its far reaches. Perhaps there was a fish of legendary proportion waiting for him. A vision of Moby Dick entered his mind, and for a moment he trembled at the thought of coming face to face with any creature of that magnitude.

As he dressed for his day on the lake, Adam became a bit giddy. He chose to wear shorts, a t-shirt, ankle socks, and his beat up pair of Nike sneakers. He also wore a swimsuit under his shorts in case he was moved to take a quick dip. Although Adam never gave it a thought, Lucci bought a tube of sun screen knowing that it would come in handy should his famous tenant decide to fish during the hottest part of the day, and be vulnerable to the scorching ultraviolet rays of the sun. He also opted to bring along a hooded sweatshirt in the event that a sudden chill would emerge on the lake.

He chose a most peculiar t-shirt to wear for the fishing trip, yet was his favorite. It was purchased in the gift shop of the New York Metropolitan Museum of Art during a special exhibit of artifacts from the reigns of Queen Hatshepsut and Cleopatra; the only female rulers of Ancient Egypt. On the front of the shirt was the *cartouche* or name plate of King Tut, the boy-king, known more for his treasures founded by Howard Carter in the Valley of the Kings, than for any accomplishments he may have attained during his brief tenure as pharaoh. The name of a person was very important to the ancient Egyptians. Without it, even at the time of death, would prevent a person from attaining eternal life. The *cartouche* included the name of the Egyptian written in hieroglyphics, and was tied around the mummy with a "magical" rope.

The study of "The Land of the Nile" intrigued Adam ever since he was a young boy, so much so, that he minored in Ancient Civilizations while at college. His interest in Egyptology filtered into a few of his novels including one of his best sellers entitled *Terror in 5703* that reflected his knowledge of the ancient and mysterious art of Egyptian mummification.

He packed away a few snacks, and in an ice chest added a couple bottles of water and cans of soda. The loon clock on the wall, now read ten o'clock. As he walked toward the shed to retrieve his fishing gear, he gazed at the loon's nest and saw that the female was still sitting atop it. The male wasn't too far away pacing up and down along the bank, and jumping in and out of the water.

After loading the boat he pushed off, and started out for a long and relaxing day on Mirror Lake. As he made his way to the middle of the lake, he enjoyed the crispness of the air, the clear blue sky, and the warmth of the early morning sun. The lake was bursting with several land and air animals, and he was excited about finding out what kind of life dwelt underwater. He had a very good feeling about what he'd be pulling out of the lake today.

When he arrived at a point that seemed to be close enough to the center of the lake, he anchored the bark, and the first thing he did was to apply sun screen on his body. He proceeded to prepare his fishing rod, choosing to use an artificial lure called a plug that was fashioned in the likeness of a minnow. It was made of hollow metal, had three separate treble hooks attached to its underbelly, and a bent frame that made it appear to be wounded. A plastic bib below its head would provide a wobbly movement as the lure was being reeled in.

Since the plug was larger and heavier than the spoon used the day before, Adam was able to cast it another twenty feet across the lake. At the precise moment the plug hit the water; it had a strike! Surprised by the quick hit, Adam nearly fell overboard, but was able to maintain his balance. He jerked the rod, and began to bring his catch home. Whatever he hooked this time, was giving him a greater fight than did the big mouth bass. Just as was the case with his prize fish of yesterday, Adam thought at one point that he had lost it. Suddenly, it took off as if it were trying one last attempt to get away. Adam held his ground, and continued to reel in the line. The fish was no match for its pursuer, tired out, and allowed itself to be reeled in the last fifteen feet giving no resistance. From out of the water, Adam pulled out a four foot muskellunge!

The fish was too long to net, so Adam pulled it into the boat. Just as he was about to lower it to the floor, the "muskie" snapped off the lure, and began pounding and flipping with great strength and determination. Adam waited for it to calm down, picked up a towel, lifted it up with two hands, and lowered the fish into the water. What a surge of adrenaline that flowed through his body!

He felt his heart beating a mile a minute, and was now gasping for air. He sat down and envisioned what the beauty would look like mounted on a wall in his home office. He was off to a great start, but wondered how he could ever top what he had just reeled in. He cracked a can of soda, and rested a bit before casting the line for a second time. He kept the same plug on the swivel, since it had brought him good luck. He stood in the boat and let go. This time, it didn't get an immediate hit, but as he slowly reeled in the line, he felt another tug. He hooked another foot long small mouth bass.

Morning quickly became afternoon, as Adam continued to pull in a wide assortment of fish including a large catfish that must have weighed over twenty pounds. This surprised him for he knew that catfish are scavengers, and like to stay at the bottom of the lake. They were more likely to be caught by a hook that had a worm or a dough ball of meal sitting motionless on the floor of the lake. It was very odd having been hooked by an artificial lure. Perhaps it was just hungry. Judging by the position of the sun in the sky, Adam guessed that it was about three o'clock. He was hot and felt the effect of the sun on his back and shoulders. He had also worked up an appetite, so stopped the sport for a bite to eat and drink. After he finished, he decided to row farther away from the cabin until he reached the opposite side of the lake from where the shanty stood. As he anchored, he looked across the lake, and could hardly see his humble abode.

He fished for an hour in the one spot, and hauled in several fish. He was amazed at their size, color and healthy appearance. He theorized that it had something to do with the water that could have a very high concentration of minerals. At this point Adam had a strong urge to swim.

The heat had taken its toll on him, and he was in need of cooling off. He had no idea of the lake's depth, so used an oar to help figure it out. It didn't touch bottom, so he knew that it was at least over his head. Adam was an excellent swimmer in his youth having the Boy Scouts of America to thank. One of the requirements to earn the rank of Eagle Scout was to acquire the three aquatic merit badges of Swimming, Canoeing and Lifesaving. He also earned the Mile Swim patch three times during summer camp, and was a member of the local YMCA where he'd swim every week.

Despite how well he swam as a boy, he wasn't very confident that he could swim very well in his old age. It didn't help that he hadn't swum for thirty years! *What is there to be afraid of? It is only a lake.* After thinking it over for a brief moment, he stripped down to his swimsuit, and was ready to take the plunge.

As he dove from the vessel and hit the water, a rush of refreshing coolness shot throughout his entire parched body. He quickly came to the surface and took a full breath of air. He chose to swim away from the boat. It was very invigorating! He decided to submerge, and open his eyes hoping that he'd be able to see what was on the other side of the mirror. He was stunned by the clarity of the water, and was able to see more than he had imagined. He rose to the surface, took another deep breath and went down again. A colorful school of fish, a hundred-strong, swam by him. He estimated that the bottom of the lake was thirty feet from the surface. He was impressed by the rich amount of colorful vegetation that covered its floor, as well as how far he could see clearly in all directions.

He rose to the surface again, and swam further away from the boat. He challenged himself by swimming to the bottom of the lake holding his breath for as long as he could, and then returning to the surface for air. The more he went through his routine, the easier it seemed to get. He couldn't believe what he was able to accomplish knowing that he hadn't swum, or performed any exercise for as long as he could remember! He swam for forty-five minutes without tiring or cramping. He finally returned to the boat, and hung on its side while still predominantly in the lake. As he looked into the skiff, a frightening thought entered his mind, *How am I ever going to get back in without tipping the boat over?* He took a deep breath and taking a firm grip on the side of the boat with both hands, tried to lift his left leg out of the water and fling it inside. He failed in his first attempt and in his second as well. At the third try, he was able to get one foot into the boat, but struggled to manage any other part of his leg or body into it.

Suddenly, he felt someone or something take hold of his body that pushed him over the side and into the boat. He lay petrified with fear for a moment, until he garnered the courage to peek over the side of the boat and look into the lake. To his utter amazement, he spied a beautiful woman with long red hair and piercing emerald-colored eyes smiling at him. A few feet from where her head, neck, and shoulders were sticking out of the water, was a split fin that Adam had only seen in the movies or read in books of fantasy. He had been helped by a mermaid!

Chapter Eight

It Must Be Something in the Water

The befuddled man rubbed his eyes, as if his underwater swim had impaired his vision. He slowly opened them expecting to see a large tree branch sticking out of the water, but lo and behold; she was still there. The duo stared at each other motionless, and Adam wondered if she would begin speaking to him. Perhaps she was waiting for him to break the ice. He could only think of two words that he'd dare say to her, so as a minute passed into their stalemate; he said in a low voice, "Thank you." With these words the enchanting creature, half woman and half fish, nodded and gracefully submerged into the depths of lake; head first followed by her tail. He was awestruck as he watched the human form of her lower body change into a beautiful emerald-green, and then into a variety of hues until the tail became a spectacular shade of turquoise. It glistened with hundreds of translucent diadems that when stuck by a beam of light burst into a plethora of colors.

Adam, now trembling, slowly lifted himself from the bottom of the boat, and sat on the wooden plank that served as a seat. He took a clean towel and wiped himself off, as his eyes never left the place where he had seen the mermaid. After a brief moment, he was finally able to gather his composure and breathed not a sigh of relief, but one of disbelief. *Could this be a dream? How can this lake make me see things that I have never before seen, or things that human eyes shouldn't behold at all?*

He looked into the lake, and just as what had been the case other times; he saw nothing but his own reflection. As if the mermaid wasn't enough, the man he saw in the lake wasn't Adam Tiller! He saw a different man; one who seemed much younger. The image frightened him, so he quickly lifted his head making a strange noise, as if gasping for air. What made the reflection he saw even more bizarre was that he also felt younger. *Is it something in the water that has caused this change, or am I going insane?* It was too much for him to comprehend.

It didn't take very long for the warmth of the sun to dry him completely. He feared getting a bad case of sunburn, as the hot rays of the sun were beginning to sting his shoulders. He threw on his t-shirt and thought of rowing back to the cabin, but chose to stay in the hope of seeing the enchantress one more time. He wanted to do a bit more fishing, but the horrible thought of hooking her entered his mind. He imagined the reaction of Vincent Peale, if he chose to tell him the story of the mermaid.

He'd never believe me, and wonder if I was a candidate for the funny farm! Yet, could Adam blame his publisher? It was hard believing such a story despite having seen the mermaid himself! He smiled as he imagined telling Peale, *Yeah, you should have seen the one that got away!* If Adam had been drinking all day, he could easily explain what he had seen. It would have been a hallucination; however, he hadn't consumed a drop of alcohol. He really did see her!

He cracked open a cold soda, and enjoyed the bubbly sensation as it traveled down his dry throat. He drank the entire twelve ounce can without coming up for air. He hadn't performed a similar feat since he was a kid. Maybe he *was* getting younger. He elected to pull up anchor, and move elsewhere on the lake to fish. It was too beautiful a day to head back to the cabin, and besides he might be visited again by his new friend. He fished for three more hours hauling in one prize fish after another. He could count on one hand the number of casts in which he came up empty. There was no doubt in his mind that Mirror Lake was magical. In all the days and nights that he would fish, never once would he have a bad fishing day. He wasn't going to be the guy who'd come home after a fishing trip to tell his buds, "All that I caught was a cold!" Fishing in Mirror Lake was like no other fishing trip that Adam Tiller had ever taken in his entire life, and the *best* catch still lay ahead!

The angler had long finished all the food and drink that he had brought with him, and was beginning to get hungry. He looked at the position of the sun in the sky, and estimated that it had to be close to six p.m. Despite the time, he still didn't want to return to the cabin because he wanted to see his new friend one more time. The excellent fishing also made him want to stay until dark, and of course there would be another glorious sunset to enjoy. It didn't take much time for Adam to convince himself to spend a couple more hours on the lake, even if it meant that he'd grow more hungry and thirsty. It was well worth the wait for he hooked another muskie that was longer than the one he caught yesterday. It seemed as if the sunset was more spectacular than the previous two nights, as he sat with mouth agape taking in the kaleidoscope of changing colors. As the moon and stars replaced the sun and clouds in the sky, Adam knew it was time to be heading back. There would be no more mermaid sightings tonight, but every time he'd return to the lake; it would be with the anticipation of seeing her again.

He paddled back to the cabin with the greatest of ease. He sailed straight across the entire width of the lake without having to stop a single time to rest. He moored the vessel, and returned the fishing gear to the shed after rinsing it off. He noticed how much his skin reddened as he showered, and hoped that he wouldn't feel the sunburn's ill-effects later in the evening. When he returned to the cabin, he put on a fresh set of clothes, started up the fire, and before beginning to prepare for dinner chose to shave.

He walked into the bathroom, turned on the water, and looked into the mirror. He dropped the can of shave cream in his hand, as his bottom jaw lowered in disbelief. What he had seen in the lake was true. He was a different man. There were now, more black strands of hair on his head than there were white ones. The black circles and puffy bags under his eyes were gone. He searched for a number of age spots that he knew were on his face, arms, and legs. They, too, had miraculously vanished, and best of all, there wasn't a single wrinkle on his face. Adam Tiller appeared twenty years younger! He sat on the toilet seat absolutely flabbergasted. He was mystified by all that was happening to him, yet he was likewise quite jubilant. *Could I have found Ponce de Leon's legendary Fountain of Youth . . . but in Wisconsin?*

He somehow found the strength to shave his now, middle-aged face. He wondered if this remarkable change was only going to be short-lived. *Will I wake up tomorrow morning as my usual old self?* Only time would tell, but for the present he'd try to process what had occurred to him over the last few hours. One thing was for certain; his sudden metamorphosis also had an enormous effect on his appetite.

For dinner, he breaded chicken cutlets that he'd fry and eat with a baked potato, corn, and what was left of last night's salad. Preparing meals were now, as much fun as eating them. He mused on how this sort of enjoyment had suddenly taken over him. Up until a couple of nights ago, he hated to cook, but now, it had become a more pleasant experience. Adam was indeed a changed man, and in more ways than one. He toyed with ordering a number of baking products, so he could tackle baking a cake, brownies, or a home-made apple pie. As he looked at what he had prepared for dinner, it didn't seem to be enough. He boiled a pot of water, added the other half pound of pasta, and heated the rest of the tomato sauce. He also threw in what was left of the loaf of garlic bread. He couldn't remember the last time he had eaten so much, yet without feeling bloated. *Maybe twenty years ago?* He spent well over two hours preparing, eating, and cleaning up after the meal. Oddly, none of it seemed to have bothered him. He was savoring the time given him in the northwoods of Wisconsin, and was enjoying every second of it. *It has to be something in the water to have brought upon these peculiar changes in me.*

It was on this night, the third one at Mirror Lake, when Adam decided to write a daily journal. He stroked up the fire, poured a glass of fruit juice, and with laptop in hand, settled on the recliner. He had to go back to "Day One," and write all that he had experienced from the very beginning, as well as adding his own personal reflections. He wrote effortlessly and with great excitement. By time he completed the third day, he had produced thirty pages of writing. After he finished the entries for the first three days, he put his laptop on the floor beside him and sat back into a more comfortable position. He smiled, feeling satisfied with the dinner he put together, but more for what he had written.

It was at this juncture that the esteemed best selling author arrived at an idea for his new book. It would be about his stay at Mirror Lake. He knew that no one would ever believe his remarkable story in real life, so why not write a story about his experience, and call it a fantasy? Adam grinned from ear to ear having just found a new genre and a most original story. He decided to call his book *Miracle on Mirror Lake.* His target audience would be adults, particularly those who were in need of a second chance in life. *Everyone needs to look into a mirror during their life. If the person doesn't like the reflection then, he or she must make an effort to change! It is never too late in life to become, to be happy, or to find love and meaning.* Unlike his other novels, this one required no research; for all the necessary information was taken from the northwoods of Wisconsin, and on a most enchanting lake. But most of all, the greatest source of inspiration would be found in the heart and soul of Adam Tiller.

He closed his eyes and began to relive the three days he had just written about in his journal. He recalled the natural beauty of the surroundings with its abundant and diverse flora and fauna. In his thoughts he reeled in the big mouth bass and muskie once again. He tasted the dinners he had whipped up the last two nights, breathed the fresh air of his walk in the woods, and saw the beautiful mermaid that had helped him get back into the boat. Most of all, he tried to arrive at an explanation of his sudden return to a younger and healthier man. He laughed to himself asking, *What could ever top my first three days at Mirror Lake?* He wouldn't be upset if all the magic would suddenly come to an end because he, now, had a story. He would simply use his imagination and creative writing skills to craft the rest of the story, even if he would never have another day like the one he experienced today. Yet, there was something deep inside him that made him think that it was only the beginning. This gut feeling would prove to be no fluke, or a mere case of wishful thinking. There was more in store for the rejuvenated author; more mystifying experiences and changes that would occur both around him and within him. For Adam Tiller, it was only the tip of the iceberg.

In the middle of reliving the phenomenal start of his four month stay at Mirror Lake, he fell asleep. Even if he was twenty years younger, and apparently in better physical shape, all that Adam had experienced today was enough to take its toll on even the youngest and most healthy person. For some unknown reason, he awoke at two a.m., and chose to sleep in the bedroom for the first time. He rose from the recliner, and secured the windows and doors before retiring. As he was heading for the bedroom, he heard a loud banging noise coming from the backyard. He realized that it may have been what may have awakened him. He picked up a broom from a corner of the kitchen, and left the lodge from the front door. He heard the noise again, and concluded that someone or something was rummaging through the two trash cans behind the cabin. He wasn't sure if he should make his way behind the cabin, or go back and lock himself in.

Giving little thought, he opted to continue around the side of the cabin to the backyard. As he slowly turned the corner his heart was racing, and his lungs were taking quick shallow breaths of air. He was, now, face to face with a black bear that wasn't supposed to be found in this section of the northwoods! He stood motionless, hoping that it would be too busy in the trash cans to notice him. He felt silly holding a broom, as if it was going to defend him against a hungry five hundred pound charging black bear. He didn't think that the bear was very old, and upon a closer look, it surely wasn't five hundred pounds. This made him feel more at ease, but then, the thought of Mama and Papa bears coming along in search of Baby bear, filled Adam with a greater fear.

There was nothing in the *Boy Scout Handbook* that offered advice in the situation of a scout coming face to face with a bear, yet he thought that the best thing to do was to keep as still and quiet as possible. He imagined having heard someone once say, *Stand still, and whatever you do, don't run!* It may not have been related to black bears, but he still thought it was good advice given his position. It seemed like an eternity to Adam, yet he waited patiently. Suddenly, as if the bear heard a gun shot, or its mother calling, stopped what it was doing, and dashed into the woods. Adam breathed a sigh of relief. He made an about-face, and headed back inside. He added one last entry to his journal for "Day Three," and finally went to bed wondering if he'd ever see the black bear again, or worse, its *Mama and Papa*. If he did, it would be the last bowl of porridge, or any meal whatsoever that he'd be eating at Mirror Lake; even a grand meal similar to what he had put together earlier in the evening.

Chapter Nine

Aunt Bea

For the next two weeks Adam maintained the daily regimen of walking through the woods in the morning, and fishing in the afternoon until dusk. He also wrote a daily entry in his journal, and read a few pages of *Moby Dick* before retiring. He hadn't seen the enchanting mermaid during this time, nor did he have any other unusual experiences. He developed a dark tan that made him appear healthier, and continued to look twenty years younger. He hadn't taken a swim in the lake in fear of what he might see, or what might happen to him.

In the middle of enjoying the sunset in his boat on an evening during the third week at Mirror Lake, another remarkable occurrence took place. While eating a peanut butter and jelly sandwich, the boat suddenly was tossed around by a large wake that came out of nowhere. Adam surveyed his surroundings, expecting to see a large ship pass that would have been the cause of the wake, but the only vessel on the lake was his own. As sudden as it arose, the wake stopped, and calm returned beneath him. From about fifty feet away another wake began to move in his direction. As the disturbance approached the skiff, it instantly subsided. *Something must have passed under the boat—something really big!* No lake fish could have had such an effect on the water; not even the largest pike that could reach five feet in length.

Adam began to reel in the fishing line, and was relieved that there didn't seem to be anything hooked. When the line returned to the boat, he saw that the night crawler was at the end of the hook and still intact. The lake was no help in ascertaining what had just passed under the skiff; for all it did was reflect whatever was above it. He began to fear what it may have been, so he picked up an oar ready to defend himself. *Some weapon!* He saw the wake reappear, and begin to circle the boat about thirty feet away while slowly spiraling closer to it. A cold sweat overcame him, and his heart began pumping harder and harder. Closer and closer . . . harder and harder. The vessel was being tossed about like a toy boat in a child's bath tub. He knew that whatever was beneath him would soon be revealing itself. He swallowed hard, and braced himself for the worse.

The movement in the water ceased for a short time, and then started up again directly in front of him about fifty feet away. Whatever it was, it seemed to have been playing a game with Adam. The thought of Moby Dick swallowing him alive shot through his mind, and caused him to shiver. The wake once again began to move in the direction of the vessel, and Adam felt that the end was near. When only ten feet from the boat, the wake was replaced by a bubbling sensation. It was as if the lake had become a cauldron of boiling liquid. Finally, the creature decided to reveal its identity. Out of the bubbling water emerged a giant behemoth; an amphibious monster with smooth skin the color of a pink rose and speckled in black. It was all neck except for its head that had two rounded horns at the top between two small ears. It had two tiny holes for nostrils, and a relatively small mouth. At least Adam wouldn't have to worry about being swallowed whole!

Of all its facial features, the one that was most outstanding was the piercing aquamarine eyes that blinked, as it stared curiously at him. It didn't seem to be sinister at all; in fact Adam would later call it *cute* in his daily journal. It was the type of benevolent creature that one would read in a children's fantasy book; rather than in a young adult's Gothic horror novel. Suddenly, the eyes of the behemoth closed, and a strong puff of sweetly-scented air was discharged from its nostrils knocking off Adam's fishing hat. "Bless you," he said with a faint smile on his face. He slowly picked up half of his peanut butter and jelly sandwich, and held it in the air hoping that it would take the snack as a peace offering. He gestured for it to be taken, and after having inspected it quite thoroughly; the creature took the sandwich gently from his hand.

Adam giggled as he imagined the treat sticking somewhere in its long neck, and then feared that the monster would be upset for giving it such a hard thing to swallow. Adam thought it would have been better to offer the carton of night crawlers! The gargantuan lifted its head, and peered into the sky providing a straighter path to its stomach. It made a queer sound that Adam interpreted as one of delight. A few seconds later, it slowly sunk back into the lake. He thought that it winked at him before its head finally caught up with its neck, but shook it off as only being his imagination.

It had been over two weeks since Adam had seen the mermaid that he had named Ariel, and now, something even more spectacular had paid him a visit. *What on earth is going on around here?* A*nd what kind of world have I stumbled upon?* He was certain that Lucci knew of this place, but why hadn't he been given a heads up? It surely wasn't a place for the weak of heart. He would later write the proprietor a note, and attach it to the grocery list. Adam amused himself thinking what he might order from the grocery store for his new-found friend. *Dog biscuits?* He concluded that the behemoth had lived here for a long time without any assistance, so chose to forgo any special treats for it.

It was time to head back to the shanty. Adam couldn't wait to type the day's entry in his journal. It seemed as if he rowed back in record time. He quickly put away the fishing gear, showered, and sank into the recliner with laptop in hand rearing to punch in the magnificent details. In light of the fabled Loch Ness monster affectionately being given the nickname of *Nessie,* he thought that it would be a neat idea to give his discovery, one as well. Since the first word that came to his mind when he saw the beast was "behemoth," he began to mull over a number of nicknames that started with the letter "B." Since it wasn't a terrorizing monster, but more like a pet; he chose to give it a friendly name. It was pink in color, so he assumed that it was female. Its eyes were more loving than they were menacing. After some consideration of a few possibilities, he picked the name "Aunt Bea." At least it was a tad more original than the name he had chosen for the mermaid. After he typed in its name, he recalled *The Andy Griffith Show* that he watched as a young boy in the sixties. Andy's paternal aunt played by seasoned actress, Frances Bavier, was named "Aunt Bee." *Well, the name isn't so original after all, but it doesn't matter for I really like it. Aunt Bea, it is going to be.*

As he sat on the porch after dinner, Adam looked at the lake, and was hedging with the idea of taking another plunge tomorrow. Would he see Aunt Bea or Ariel? Conceivably, there was a strange new world awaiting him that no set of human eyes had ever beheld. Part of him shivered with the fear of the unknown. Suppose there were unfriendly creatures waiting to devour him? Yet another part of him was full of wonder and awe, and a sense of innate curiosity. After having typed eight pages to describe his encounter with Aunt Bea it was time to hit the sack.

He thought that it was rather odd to find that he was reading a few more pages of *Moby Dick,* after having come face to face with his own behemoth. About a hundred pages into the book, he heard was startled by a loud banging sound that was coming from the back of the cabin. This time, its source wasn't the metal trash cans, so he ruled out "The Three Bears." Besides, he moved the cans into one of the sheds to assure that his garbage wouldn't be attracting any more animals. In light of what he had seen in the lake, he pondered if it was the legendary Bigfoot or the Jersey Devil. He laughed after reminding himself that he was in the northwoods of Wisconsin, and not in the pinelands of New Jersey! As he opened the door in his bedroom, a burst of wind forced its way in, bringing with it leaves, twigs, and other small pieces of debris. For the first time since Adam had come to Mirror Lake, he was about to experience a violent storm.

He closed the door, and quickly put on his sweat suit and sneakers. He was glad that it hadn't begun to rain, and hoped to secure things before it started to pour. He found the source of the noise; a door on one of the sheds had sprung open. He closed the door and locked it. He sped over to the other shed, secured it as well, and ran over to tie the boat more tightly to the dock. He looked toward the lake, and saw a flash of light in the sky that was followed by the roar of thunder. He heard the strike of a lightning bolt, and was certain that a tree had been struck somewhere in the woods behind the cabin.

Large drops of rain fell on his head and shoulders, so he hurried back to the porch, and brought the rocking chair and table into his safe haven. He saw the bass-thermometer swaying back and forth on the wooden post, so chose to also bring it inside. It started to rain heavily amidst the continuous crackle of lightning and the roar of thunder. Adam gazed over at the loon's nest, debating if it would survive the torrential rainfall and strong gusty wind. *If only I could bring it into the safety of the cabin. I mustn't worry for Nature takes care of its own.*

For the next couple of hours, he waited out the storm. Sheets of rain pounded the roof of the cabin that made an unnerving noise. The wind howled like an angry banshee, and at times lashed violently against the windows. The lights throughout the cabin flickered. Although worried, Adam was impressed by how well the cabin was standing up against such severe elements. At times, he'd sit in bed reading his book, and then he'd go on the porch to watch the storm more closely. The thought of a flash flood crossed his mind. *What will I do if the water suddenly begins to rise? I don't think Lucci will be coming to my rescue. Besides, even if he or his son would try, the roads could be flooded out, making any rescue attempt virtually impossible.*

As midnight approached, Adam saw that the storm was starting to lighten up. He breathed a sigh of relief, as the sheets of rain became large drops, and then just a drizzle. He knew that there was no longer any need to worry; however, there was still one concern that he had—the loon's nest. He took a flashlight that was stored under the kitchen sink, and from the porch directed its beam to the birch tree. The nest was gone! Not being concerned with the light rainfall, but for the safety of the loons, Adam walked slowly toward the tree. He looked at its base and several feet around it, but found no evidence of the nest, eggs, or birds. He returned to the dwelling saddened by the dismal prospect that all were lost. He dried off, and had a light snack before returning to his book. He was relieved that he had weathered a nasty storm, and had not encountered Bigfoot. Yet, he wondered if he'd ever see his feathered-friends again.

Chapter Ten

Nature Takes Care of Its Own

Adam woke up at ten in the morning, put on a pot of coffee, and inspected the area around the cabin for damage. There were a number of limbs that had fallen from trees and some light debris that had collected in the backyard, but there was no structural damage to the cabin, sheds, or shower stall. A few cedar logs blew off the chord, so he returned them to the pile. The channel didn't seem any higher, and he was relieved that there wasn't any evidence of flooding. The boat was still moored to the dock, and neither had sustained any damage. He set up the table and rocking chair on the porch, and hung the thermometer to the post. He returned to the cabin, poured a mug of fresh-brewed coffee, and ate a bowl of cereal with a sliced banana. He cut up an apple, placed it in a bowl, and sat on the porch.

There was freshness in the air that he attributed to the rain. He listened to the sweet sound of birds singing their morning melodies. As he looked at the birch tree, he speculated about the loons that were driven violently from their home by the severe storm. He gazed into the channel hoping to see the expectant father swimming up and down. Suddenly, he caught something from the corner of his eye. A small animal was approaching him from the opposite side of the porch. He slowly turned his head in its direction, so not to spook it, and discovered that it was a small fawn; probably the one that he had seen a couple of weeks ago upon his return from the walk in the woods. *Was it separated from its parents during the storm, or did they desert the poor animal in a panic?*

He slowly picked up an apple slice from the bowl, and held it out in front of him. He waited patiently hoping that the fawn would trust him and take it from his hand. The fawn warily walked closer to Adam, and gently took the apple from his hand. Adam took another slice, and this time, placed it on the palm of his hand. The young deer once again took it. As it approached for the third time, Adam gently placed his hand on its neck, and moved it along its back. He was surprised by the fawn's docility. After the animal had its fill, it left the porch and made its way back into the woods. As the days passed at Mirror Lake, the fawn visited each morning expecting to be fed.

As was the case with the other creatures both natural and unusual that became part of Adam's outdoor experience, Adam chose to give each one of them a name. The deer was certainly not going to be nick-named *Bambi*, so he pondered a more original name for his newest friend.

He resolved that it would be called *Storm,* for it was the storm that had brought it to him.

When Adam went back inside, he was still hungry so made an egg omelet, home-fried potatoes, and Philadelphia scrapple that he was glad Lucci had found at a Wisconsin supermarket. He cut thin slices from the one pound piece, and floured them before frying. He marveled again, as to how he enjoyed eating. Conceivably, all the drinking and smoking had an ill-effect on his taste buds, or maybe he hadn't taken the time to enjoy what he was eating. It could have also been a combination of the two. All Adam knew, was that he was presently enjoying life's simple pleasures, and some of the things, such as eating a home-cooked meal, or cooking that he always considered a chore, had become a joy. If Marie could only see him now.

By one o'clock, he was back on the porch deciding what to do for the rest of the day. He had already missed his walk in the woods, and wasn't sure if he wanted to fish on the morning after a storm. Suddenly, he heard a voice from within, beckoning him to take another plunge into the lake. *Am I creating these thoughts in my head, or has the lake taken control of me?* He was apprehensive to take a swim in light of the storm, wondering if it in some way had disrupted the lake's friendly confines.

Before having made a final decision, he gazed in the direction of the birch tree, and became ecstatic when he saw that the two loons had returned, yet this time with four additional members of their family! Somehow, they were able to survive the storm. The chicks were gray puffs of cotton, and looked nothing like their parents. *Nature does take care of its own.* He speculated how they had managed to escape the violence of the storm. *Did the eggs hatch before or after the storm? If the former is true, their instinct could have alerted them to the upcoming danger, and give them time to seek shelter.* He watched in delight as the fledglings followed their mother in a straight line from the birch tree to the channel. It was time for their first swimming lesson. Adam laughed as he saw each of the youngsters struggle at times to stay afloat, and paddle their way from one side of the channel to the other. The once-anxious dad did little than watch his mate do all the work, yet if it could feel anything on a human level; he had to be bursting with pride.

Acknowledging that nature provides for its own, Adam still had an urge to feed the new family. He didn't want to disrupt the swimming lesson, so nixed the idea for the time being. Quite satisfied with the side show, he returned to his previous debate over whether or not to take the plunge. After a few minutes of thought, he opted to take a walk in the woods. He made a quick change of clothing that included a new set of hiking boots that he had ordered last week. He also bought a nylon knapsack, so he could bring along a few sacks and bottled water for longer hikes.

His promenade in the woods had evolved into a hike, and took longer than when he had first started. He grew less tired, and ventured off onto alternative trails. He had grown confident in his hiking skills, and no longer feared getting lost. He made very few rest stops along the way, and covered several miles a day. He made it a point to stop and study something more closely, or to watch an animal at work or play. He felt like a new man, a Rocky Balboa, who had reached the top of the Philadelphia Art Museum after having scaled its many steps at the end of his long run across the city. He felt one with nature, and repeatedly was able to experience the same euphoria that he enjoyed while fishing on the lake.

When he returned to his hovel, he looked for the loons, but they were nowhere to be found. He wondered if mom decided to take them out into the lake for a more challenging swim. He sat on the porch for a short time enjoying the satisfaction of having hiked for what he estimated to have been about ten miles. He grabbed a bottle out of the knapsack, took a refreshing sip, and poured the rest over his head. He took a deep breath and smiled. Coming to Mirror Lake was one of the best choices that he had ever made in his life. Maybe even the best! He had no idea what was happening to him, but he knew one thing; he didn't want it to end. He had a gut feeling that it wasn't over. He knew that he could go further. There was no stopping him now.

It was time to write the grocery list for Lucci's son. It also gave him the opportunity to share his experiences that would warrant a response, if not an explanation of what has been going on. He didn't know where to begin, as he sat at the kitchen table with pen and notebook in hand. He gathered his thoughts and began to write a letter.

Dear Lucci,

Before you left me almost three weeks ago, you told me that when I'd leave Mirror Lake, that I'd never be the same. I, now know, what you meant!

It is imperative that I speak to you as soon as possible.

I have seen things at the lake, wonderful things, that no one except, you, could ever believe. I am sure that you have seen them, too.

I am looking forward to your visit.

Sincerely,

Adam Tiller

P.S. Whatever is a treat for loons and deer, please add it to my grocery list.

He also wanted to add "friendly behemoths" to his postscript, as well as "beautiful mermaids." He also toyed with the idea of requesting several jars of honey for "The Three Bears," but chose otherwise. He folded the letter, placed it in a sealed envelope, and wrote the proprietor's name on it. He completed the weekly grocery list, and put both envelopes under the door mat. He hoped that Lucci would come over in the next couple of days, but the call of the lake was getting stronger. He was able to resist it earlier, but he wasn't sure how much longer he could hold out. He was certain there was something else that Mirror Lake wanted to show him. By the time he returned to the kitchen, he decided that he was going to take the plunge tomorrow.

He read a couple hundred pages of *Moby Dick*, and fell asleep with Aunt Bea on his mind; rather than the great white whale. He couldn't in his wildest dreams, imagine what was in store for him when he'd, once again, venture into the depths of the lake's magical waters. He wasn't aware at the moment that he was at the threshold of making the most momentous discovery of his life, and arguably, in all of human history; one that would impress even the courageous Captain Ahab.

Chapter Eleven

The Secret of Mirror Lake

Adam was up bright and early wanting to get back into his daily routine. He chose to no longer drink coffee wanting to cut down on his intake of caffeine. He was now, more health-conscious than he had ever been at any time in his life. He felt great, and wanted it to remain with him after his departure from Mirror Lake. He was given his life back, and was determined to take better care of it. He ate a bowl of cereal with blueberries, along with a glass of orange juice. He packed an apple, a bag of trail mix, and a couple bottles of spring water. The day of eating potato chips and other snacks loaded with oily fats, carbs, and cholesterol was over. He slipped into his hiking attire and was off. Although he knew that he could walk at a faster rate, Adam chose to take a slower pace; still wanting to absorb all that nature had to offer. It was more important to connect with nature, his Maker and with himself, than to gain an entry in the *Guinness Book of World Records*.

Instead of unhealthy snacks, he packed in the knapsack, two nature manuals that he found on the bookcase. It would help him to identify unfamiliar plant and animal life. He took a different trail on this particular morning, and stopped a couple of times to check his nature manual. He was surprised when he came upon a very tall American holly tree. He thought that this plant, used by his wife to decorate the mantel over the fireplace and window ledges at Christmas, came only in the form of a small bush. He also was able to identify the Eastern Redbud, and the magnificent Sugar Maple. He was delighted to recognize a number of birds including a Red-headed woodpecker, and a small songbird called the Boreal chickadee. He couldn't wait to take the manuals with him on the boat to identify the abundant flora and fauna that inhabited the lake.

During the hike he came upon a creek that he followed for about a mile and that opened a whole new world of land and water creatures, including a nest of frog eggs, as well as a number of tadpoles. At one point, he took off his socks and hiking boots to walk in the water. He could have easily spent the rest of the afternoon hiking along the waterway, turning over rocks and logs, but he knew that he had an important appointment with Mirror Lake. After a couple hours of hiking and exploring he started back to the cabin with a new appreciation for nature. *What is happening to me? I never cared much about such things. Oh, the joy of stopping to smell the roses!*

There was no need to shower or change any of his clothes. He slipped his swimsuit under his hiking shorts, and put on his old pair of sneakers. He gathered a few *healthy* snacks, and filled the cooler with ice and bottled water. He rounded up his fishing equipment, and headed out for the lake. He rowed to its center, anchored, and prepared the fishing rod. He chose a black spinner that had a bright red feather at the end. He cast out, and after waiting a few seconds for the lure to sink deeper into the water, began to slowly reel in the line. He could feel the movement of the lure's metal tab spinning as it was being pulled toward the boat. He wasn't as lucky as he had been before by hooking a fish on the first cast. In fact, he wasn't lucky at all. He spent an hour using a variety of artificial lures, as well as night crawlers, but nothing produced even a light nibble. He had fished here before and had brought in several fish, but it wasn't the case today. Something just wasn't right.

Did the storm have an ill-effect on the lake? Adam was now, more apprehensive to take the plunge. He was sure that Lucci would be coming tomorrow morning, so wanted to give him more information about the underwater world of Mirror Lake. Perhaps there was something more spectacular than a mermaid and a friendly leviathan waiting for him. Yet, what could possibly top this parlay? Whatever would be decided, it would be determined over lunch.

He ate a tuna wrap, an apple, and gulped a bottle of spring water. He remembered what his mother said when he was a boy vacationing along the Jersey shore, *You should never go back into the water after you eat. You have to first digest your food.* He moved to another part of the lake and continued to fish. It seemed that the change in position made a big difference, as he reeled in a few fish within minutes. He surmised that the lake needed to settle before returning to normal.

Adam rowed further away from the cabin. It helped to burn off some of the calories, and to digest his lunch. He fished for another half hour, and hauled in the usual abundance of fish. He used an oar to check for depth, and deemed that it was safe to dive into the lake from the boat. He shed his t-shirt and shorts, and slipped out of his socks and sneakers. Unlike the last time, he felt more confident going into the water, and knew that he could have a more prolonged and deeper swim. He stood up, took a deep breath, and took the plunge.

The water seemed to be a bit cooler than during the last swim, but after a few seconds, his body adjusted to the quick chill. He guessed that the temperature change was due to the storm that had stirred the water. He was surprised that although he was farther from the deepest part of the lake, he couldn't see the bottom this time. Again, it must have been due to the storm. Swimming deeper into the lake, he was thrilled to see a vast variety of colorful fish that didn't seem to have been affected by it. After having been underwater for about a minute and a half, he rose to the surface and filled his lungs with air. *I haven't been able to hold my breath this long since I was in my twenties!* He then, submerged again, but this time even deeper. He was spellbound as a huge turtle swam by him. He had seen smaller turtles sticking their heads out of the water, but never did he imagine that there were any as large as this one. For a brief time, he delighted swimming alongside the turtle, but again had to surface.

He swam further away from the boat, and when he reached the bottom of the lake, he was awestruck by the new-found clarity of the water. He could easily see at least a hundred yards in every direction. He noticed the abundant and colorful vegetation that carpeted the floor of the lake, and was thrilled to spy a large muskie, that didn't seem to be bothered by Adam's intrusion. Suddenly, he saw Ariel, who was motioning him to follow her! He swiftly moved toward her, bringing a huge smile to her face. She took him by the hand, and together they swam further away from the boat. He couldn't hold his breath much longer, so began to pull away from her. The mermaid knew exactly what to do. She moved closer to him, and after looking into his eyes for a few seconds, gave him a kiss; filling his lungs with oxygen in the process. They continued to swim hand in hand, until they arrived at their destination-an underwater cavern.

Ariel signaled for Adam to surface. He was able to climb out of the water onto rocks that were set firmly on the beach. He picked himself up, and turned to his escort who was smiling and pointing in the vicinity of a large opening in the cavern. Apparently, she wanted him to leave her and enter it. He had no other choice than to follow her gesture, but before making his way to the opening said, "Lady, you better be here when I get back!" She giggled and nodded as if she understood. This raised Adam's confidence level a few notches.

As he made his way to the entrance of the cavern, he had a strange feeling that he was walking into uncharted territory; the likes of which human eyes had never seen. Up until this point, nothing about the lake was malevolent, so

Adam didn't expect anything would hurt him or at least he hoped. The walk in which he was about to take was one that he'd never forget. He was about to discover the secret of Mirror Lake.

The wet rocky ground wasn't easy on his bare feet, but as he entered the opening, it became a plush carpet of green grass. The rock formations around him were soon transformed into rows and rows of trees and shrubs that he couldn't identify without his nature manuals. Yet, he wasn't sure if they could be found there. The darkness of the cavern gave way to a spectacular array of colors, similar to those that filled his eyes during sunset on the lake. As he walked more deeply into the cavern, it now became a kingdom. Adam conjectured that this subterranean area of Mirror Lake could be a portal into another dimension, a lost world, or perhaps a new one.

Multi-colored birds flew in the air along with other creatures that he did not recognize. He could only describe them as nymphs or fairies that glowed with a radiant light and sang beautiful melodies. Flowers of every shape, size and color sprung up around him, as if the touch of his feet somehow had pressed a growth button. Suddenly, a herd of miniature winged-white horses, no larger than beagles, sped by him! He pondered if this unusual place was a world of extinct flora and fauna, or a world not yet discovered. *Perhaps creatures, such as Ariel and Aunt Bea, swam into these enchanted waters and were trapped here. Or maybe they have always been here.* As he strolled along, Adam continued to conjure up more possible theories, yet could not arrive at any definite answers. He laughed to himself as he thought about searching for a figure like the

Wizard of Oz, who could give him some explanation of this mysterious place.

He had easily journeyed two miles along the green carpet before he came to an awareness that this place could go on forever. He decided to turn around and start back to the where he hoped Ariel would be waiting. He jumped as a brown furry critter scurried across his path from one side to the other. It looked like a ground hog, but had a white stripe riding down its back, and four white claws. He was expecting to see a unicorn, but as he came to the end of his trek, he concluded that this world was not one of fantasy, but some kind of real world! He approached the opening of the cavern, and as he departed, felt the wet rocky soil under his feet once again. He turned to take one last look at this strange world and while doing so, came to the realization that despite the abundant life that filled it, he had not seen any people. *How very strange that there is no one to enjoy this beautiful place?*

As he neared the pool of water from which he emerged, he smiled, wondering if a mermaid could qualify as being considered a person. He was relieved when she suddenly surfaced, wearing the same smile that she bore when he had left her. He smiled back at her, and whether she understood or not said, "Ariel, I had no idea! Now, please take me back to my boat." She made a hand gesture for Adam to join her in the water. She gracefully dove into the water, and the bewildered writer followed suit. Surprisingly, it didn't require another kiss to get from the cavern to the boat. This disappointed Adam. He surfaced and grabbed onto the side of the boat. This time, he needed no assistance getting into it. He looked back at the mermaid, and threw her a kiss. She smiled at him, and sank into the water with no splash or disturbance.

The disconcerted man took the two oars, and tirelessly made his way back to the cabin. There was no slowing down, or any rest stops. He was filled with energy that he hadn't felt since he was in high school. He was excited about what he had seen, and although he could make no sense of it, Adam couldn't wait until he would tell Lucci and be given a much-needed explanation.

Chapter Twelve

Into the Fog

*A*dam jumped out of the bark with the spunk of a teenager. He was invigorated by his swim, and never felt healthier. It had to be the water! He quickly unloaded his fishing gear and emptied the cooler. With all the exercise, he had worked up a hearty appetite. He marveled at the amount of physical activity that he was able to accomplish during the day; the long hike in the woods, all the rowing and swimming, and capped by the trek he had taken in his newly-discovered world. It was incomprehensible how he hadn't keeled over from exhaustion, or how he could have mustered up the stamina required to have exerted such energy. No matter how young he now looked and felt, he was still a man of sixty-three, or was he?

He chose to skip his usual shower for the water of Mirror Lake seemed to have its own cleansing effect that far surpassed anything soap and water could do. Although he was starving Adam took out his laptop with great anticipation, and began to type the entry for the absolutely amazing day he had. He didn't want to forget a single detail of his uncanny exploit beginning with his exotic escort, her bewitching kiss, the underwater cavern, and the strange new world. By the time he finished his reflection he had filled twenty full pages.

It was only after completing his journal that he began preparing for dinner. He stuffed and breaded two large pork chops that he'd bake in the oven. He cleaned three husks of corn that he'd boil in a pot of water, and smother with butter. He made a spinach salad to which he added sliced almonds and strawberries. He also placed a few crescent rolls on a tray to be baked a few minutes before he was ready to eat. He took out the pitcher of sun-brewed iced tea, and poured some into a tall glass of ice. He sat at the table with a mind that was as clear as a crystal ball, and a body that was free of any aches or pains. Nothing meant more to him than Mirror Lake; not even his financial portfolio, acclaimed books, fame or fortune. Nothing! After enjoying a tasteful dinner and cleaning up, he refilled his glass, and sat on the porch to relax.

He relived his experience in the underwater cavern, still perplexed by all he had seen. As the day was approaching its end, he looked toward the lake catching a glimpse of another dazzling sunset. He was certain that the sky in the new world to which he was privileged to lay eyes on, was more spectacular than any he had seen in his world. Shaking his head incredulously, Adam rose from the rocking chair, and made his way to the bedroom to read another segment of Melville's classic adventure. He sat up in bed, and devoured two hundred pages of the novel without a single yawn. What a remarkable difference reading it in the context of his situation at Mirror Lake, as compared to reading it as an assignment in a high school literature class! The temperature had dropped enough to bring a chill to the shanty, so Adam ignited the fire, and chose to sit on the recliner with a mug of hot cocoa topped with mini-marshmallows in his hand. He stared at the blaze and was mesmerized by the dancing flames. Although he was still full of tireless energy; he finally managed to fall asleep. It wouldn't be for very long.

It must have been the crackle of a burning cedar log that awakened him. His eyes opened at the same time an ember shot from a piece of wood, and hit against the side of the fireplace. The loon clock on the kitchen wall signaled that it was approaching midnight, yet he had no desire to go to bed. How could he possibly want to bring the greatest day of his life to an end? His insides were bursting, for he wanted to tell someone about all that he had seen, but who would ever believe him? Peale? No, he'd just laugh at him. *If only Marie was here?* What could he do to calm his thoughts that were racing wildly in his mind, and preventing him from falling asleep? He had no other choice than to return to the lake. Its attraction was relentless. He felt as if he, now, belonged to it.

Since it was cloudy, there was no moon shining on the lake as there had been on other nights. He elected to bring a propane lantern that he remembered seeing in the shed after he noticed a slight fog rolling in from the lake. He flipped on every light switch just in case the fog would thicken, thus making the cabin possible to locate from the lake. There was no guarantee, however, that he'd be able to find the hovel, even if he lit a huge bonfire in front of it! He was taking a big risk, but the calling of the lake could not be ignored. He was led to the boat by the lantern he held directly in front of him. He could hardly see the bark, and debated with himself for a brief time, whether or not it was a good idea going out on the lake in light of the circumstances. Finally, he chose to continue on his way, for its allurement was too irresistible. It was chillier than he had expected, so before he boarded the vessel, he returned to the cabin to put on his sweat suit. He packed a few carrots, an apple, and a couple bottles of water in the event that he would have to remain on the lake until the fog thinned out.

He set the lantern on the bow of the boat, and began to row carefully along the channel onto the lake. For a moment, he felt as if he was one of the fish that he had caught over the last few weeks. The lake served as the lure, and he, the big fish ready to be hooked. Adam was totally unaware that he had become obsessed with Mirror Lake, or perhaps, possessed by it. He was an innocent victim of its charm, beauty, and magic. He now found himself snagged; hook, line, and sinker.

He was overcome by an eerie feeling as the skiff floated onto the lake. The fog was sitting on its surface, so as long as it didn't totally engulf him, it would be fine. It seemed as if the boat was gliding through a cloud-filled sky rather than moving along a body of water. He hadn't arrived at the middle of the lake, when Adam noticed that the fog was beginning to rise, and was gradually covering the boat. He looked back at the land surrounding the lake, and started to worry as it slowly disappeared from his sight. When he looked down, he couldn't see any of his body below the waist. His imagination sparked a number of frightening things in his mind. His skin became clammy, and he began to feel an increase in his heart rate.

What was he to do? It was too late to turn back for he could no longer see the cabin. He had no idea in what direction to row, so instead of going any further, he pulled the oars out of their locks, and chose to sit it out. The stark silence of the night added to the eeriness of the experience. Even the night animals knew better not to venture into the fog. By now, he was swallowed by a dense cloud. He could hardly see the lantern that sat only a few feet away. If Ariel or Aunt Bea would have been as imprudent as Adam, and appeared before him, he wouldn't be able to see them. He had used poor judgment in coming to the lake, and was now, paying the price.

The least thing he wanted to do was to allow his imagination to take over, so he sat on the floor of the boat as comfortably as possible, and began to recite poems that he had memorized as a child. The first was *Paul Revere's Ride* by William Wadsworth Longfellow. *Listen, my children and you shall hear of the midnight ride of Paul Revere, on the eighteenth of April, in Seventy-five; hardly a man is now alive.* Then, a favorite called *The Duel* by Eugene Field. *The gingham dog and the calico cat side by side by the table sat. 'Twas half—past twelve, (and what do you think!) Nor one nor t'other had slept a wink!* After exhausting his store of poetry, he resorted to singing old songs of his childhood, like the one his mother sung to him when he couldn't sleep. It was from the movie, *Going My Way,* and made popular by Bing Crosby. *Too ra loo ra loo ral, too ra loo ra li. Too ra loo ra loo ral. That's an Irish lullaby.* He closed his eyes, singing the refrain over and over again, until he finally sung himself to sleep; just as the propane tank of the lantern had run out.

It was the brightness of the early morning sun peeking over the tall trees on the eastern side of the lake that eventually woke him up from his slumber. The fog had totally lifted, and Adam was delighted to be the witness of another sensational sunrise over Mirror Lake. He believed that the lake had watched over him throughout the threatening night. Similar to how nature protected the loons and his own parents had spent their entire lives taking the most loving care of him. More than at any other time in his adult life, Adam Tiller felt closeness to God, the greatest Protector of all created reality.

He opened a bottle of water, and sat in the boat for half an hour absorbing the sights, sounds, and fragrances of another beautiful dawn on Mirror Lake. The life that was hidden by the fog had emerged and filled the land, water, and sky. Despite how he may have felt last night, Adam was glad that he had come to the lake. Feeling a bit hungry, he ate his snack, and finished off the water. It was time to head back. What started off being an uncertain and at times nerve-racking morning, had become uneventful by evening. Upon his return to the cabin, he was glad that having the lights burning all night didn't drain the generator of its power. He knew nothing about generators and would have been totally helpless, if he came back to find that the cabin had no electricity. He recalled the recent storm, and wondered what he would have done had it knocked out the generator. He assumed that Lucci's son checked it periodically, but how would he know whether or not it needed to be fixed? Then, he remembered his cell phone. *Oh, yeah, how could I forget?* It seemed that Mirror Lake had so captivated him, that he wasn't thinking as he should, but by the same token, what he was now thinking was part of the change that he was undergoing; one that was for his benefit.

He picked up a few logs from the chord in the backyard, and set them beside the fireplace. The temperature in the cabin was comfortable, so he didn't need to strike up a fire for the moment. He wasn't hungry having munched on snacks while on the lake, but he did long for a cup of fresh-brewed coffee. Remembering the promise made, he poured a glass of orange juice instead, picked up his laptop and typed a journal entry about his latest uneventful, yet chilling experience on the lake.

When he finished, he took his daily stroll through the woods, and fished for a few hours on the lake. Although there was nothing unusual to write about, his mind was still very active, as he continued to process the secret of Mirror Lake. He wondered if it was his destiny to have come here, and if so, what he was now to do. *What is keeping Lucci? He could supply me with an explanation, and help me to arrive at whether or not I am here for a reason.*

Chapter Thirteen

A Startling Revelation

Upon his return from another phenomenal fishing experience, Adam chose to take a shower. He rounded up his towel, showering gel, flip flops, and headed out. He enjoyed the stimulating cool water bouncing off his well-tanned body. As he washed his hair, he marveled at the healthy crop that had replaced his thinning hair and receding hairline. Feeling the nubs on his face signaled that it was time for a shave. He never let his hair grow more than two inches long, nor did he like facial hair. Actually, it was Marie who couldn't tolerate it, so he remained clean-shaven for her. The only time that he did grow a beard was when he was writing a novel. This kept his wife at arm's length. He thought about growing a beard at Mirror Lake, but why would he want to look older? He was ecstatic looking twenty years younger, so chose to be free of facial hair.

He warmed a pot of water, and brought it into the bathroom. He placed a small hand towel in the water, and patted it on his face to soften his thin beard making it easier to shave. After a couple of minutes he took a can of shave cream, and before he lathered up looked into the mirror. He was astonished by what he saw. The age regression had happened again. This time, he was staring into the face of a twenty-three year old man! He stood paralyzed, as he kept his eyes fixed on the uncanny reflection of himself. *It MUST be the water!* He couldn't shave, now wanting to look older. He went into the kitchen, and prepared a pot of coffee, thus breaking his self-made promise. If there was a bottle of *Cutty Sark*, he probably would have downed it. He took a mug of coffee with him to the porch, sat down shaking his head in bewilderment, and agonized over what he was going to do. *How will I ever explain this phenomenon when I return home? No one is his right mind will ever believe me!*

On one hand he was elated about his metamorphosis. How many times in the course of his life had he wanted to be young again, or to turn back the hands of time? Yet, on the other hand, he was frightened by this second change. He assured himself that Lucci would have answers, but when would he be coming? He now faced a dilemma. Should he ever again swim in the lake, or visit the subterranean world in fear that he may return as a toddler? He had just about enough of this age regression, and wanted it to stop! Leaving Mirror Lake as a forty-three year old man would have been difficult to explain, but returning to Manhattan looking like a college graduate would be impossible!

Adam had only taken his iPhone in case of an emergency. He deemed that the present situation had qualified as a *major* emergency. He took it out of his carrying bag, searched for Lucci's number from its list of outgoing calls, and dialed it. Adam told Lucci he discovered the secret of Mirror Lake, and that he must see him today. He couldn't find the words to tell him that he was talking to a young man of twenty-three, yet he imagined that Lucci might have already figured it out. Unfortunately, Lucci was visiting a sick aunt in Minnesota, so couldn't visit until tomorrow at noon. For the first time as Mirror Lake, Adam couldn't wait to go to bed, so he could wake to finally share his remarkable story.

He rose early in the morning, and after a light breakfast took a short walk through the woods. He returned to the cabin in ample time to prepare lunch. He made a couple of tuna salad wraps that would be served with a home-made pasta salad of which he was very proud, and fresh fruit. He emptied the contents of the coffee pot after having made unusually strong coffee, and brewed a regular pot. He also prepared a fresh pitcher of sun-brewed iced tea with lemon, if Lucci would prefer a cold drink. By eleven-thirty he completed his preparation, and sat on the recliner to type his journal entry for yesterday that included his *new* look. When he finished, he sat back anticipating Lucci's reaction when he'd see him, and more importantly, the explanation he would be giving. *Why would Lucci consider renting out this cabin, knowing very well its secret? And why didn't he at least prepare me?* Adam wanted answers, and good ones!

At a minute shy of noon, Adam heard a knock on the door. He called for Lucci to come in; however, it wasn't the proprietor, but his son. Thinking that something must have happened to the old man, he asked the younger man, who he estimated to be in his mid-twenties, to join him in the living room. Having never met Lucci's son, the man would have no idea what Adam looked like, when he first arrived at Mirror Lake. There would be no unusual reaction to the writer, who had shaved forty years off his life! Adam extended his hand, and introduced himself. What the young man said in response was enough to have given *old man* Tiller a stroke. "Nice meeting you, Adam. My name is Michael Lucci. The older gentleman with whom you have spoken is my son, Thomas. I believe that I owe you an explanation." If ever Adam needed to down a bottle of *Cutty Sark*; it was now!

Adam was stunned by Lucci's revelation, and for a moment stood motionless with his mouth agape. When he finally composed himself, he invited Lucci to join him at the kitchen table. For the next hour and a half, the two men spoke about the secret of Mirror Lake. Lucci explained that the secret had been passed down to him by the previous owner, and that he had guarded the secret for fifty years. His son had protected it for fifty more. Adam was told that the world he had fallen upon was neither old nor new, but *redeemed*. He told Adam that it was created by God to give mankind a second chance. He had visited the world many times himself, and knew about the mermaid and the gentle gargantuan. He never found a single flaw in it. It was indeed, a new Garden of Eden.

Adam had a most difficult time believing Lucci's explanation. He hurled one question after another at him, but each one was answered more incredibly than the previous one. Lucci could give him no clear-cut answers; for it wasn't that *God Himself* revealed all of this to him or any of the guardians before him. It was a conclusion drawn by the first proprietor of the cabin, and had been passed down for centuries. Lucci told Adam that the guardian before him said that he must accept what he didn't comprehend, and be comfortable with the mystery. It was hard for Adam to do so. He was a man of science, and needed an explanation for everything in nature. Concerning his age regression, Lucci couldn't explain it, but speculated that it had something to do with giving a person a second chance at life. Adam could accept that, yet he couldn't understand why Lucci's son hadn't experienced age regression after he swam in the lake. All Lucci could say was, "Perhaps Thomas wasn't in need of a second chance."

When asked if he has always looked as young as he is presently, Lucci explained that he remained young for as long as he continued to swim in Mirror Lake, and that he never gets any younger than he appears at the present. This disclosure allayed Adam's fear of waking up one day as a baby sucking his thumb. Lucci shared his own soul-searching, and revealed that he left Mirror Lake for a short time; not wanting to be part of the outlandish predicament in which he found himself. While he was away, he began to age more rapidly than usual. His son became the guardian of the secret in his absence, but chose not to take advantage of the lake's power. When Thomas fell ill, Lucci returned to care for him, and has remained by his side ever since.

At first, Adam couldn't understand why the secret had to be protected. Lucci contended that if it was discovered by the wrong people, it would result in its defilement, and that mankind would lose its second chance. Adam couldn't understand that if it was created by God for man's second redemption, why hadn't it been revealed by God Himself? And how could its many guardians allow millions of people to die short of being redeemed a second time? Lucci could offer no reasonable explanation. All he'd say was that, "God works in His own time, for His own reason, and in His own way. Perhaps he is looking for the *right* couple to start anew." Lucci's speculation intrigued Adam. In a way it made some sense. It meant that only a world begotten by this *special* couple could be redeemed, thus it really wasn't for the present race. Was this the way God would bring an end to a world that seemed to be on a downward spiral in recent decades? It could be a way of letting a depraved world fizzle out on its own, so to speak, while a new and better one is born in an underwater cavern beneath Mirror Lake.

Even though it made sense on one hand, it just seemed too unfathomable to be plausible on the other. In essence, all the conversation did was to leave Adam with more questions, including the main one coming more from a theological point of view, "If what you say is true, wasn't our world already redeemed by Jesus Christ?" Lucci, once again, couldn't give a definite or reasonable answer. All he said in response related to the Unification Church, whose followers nicknamed the "Moonies," believe that Jesus Christ redeemed the world spiritually. Jesus was supposed to set up the ideal family, but was killed before he could fulfill his mission. In a "Blessing Ceremony," or a large scale marriage, conducted by the founder of the Church, Reverend Myung Moon, the couples are removed from the lineage of sinful humanity and engrafted into God's sinless lineage. Lucci was quick to add that he didn't believe this tenet of the Unification Church, yet it could conceivably be used to help explain the mystery of Mirror Lake.

Lucci went on to say that he had his fill of Mirror Lake. In the beginning when he, his wife, and son were young; life was good. Seeing his son grow older than his parents was heart wrenching. After his wife died, he had no other support. He decided to leave Mirror Lake, age gracefully, and die a normal death. His son understood, and became the lake's sole guardian. When he fell ill with cancer, Lucci returned to care for him. His eyes began to water as he told Adam that the cancer had spread throughout his entire body, and that he only had a few months to live. After his death, Lucci hoped to pass on the guardianship to someone else, thus the reason for advertising the property in travel magazines. Lucci admitted that he was hoping that Adam would become its new guardian, so Lucci could return to the *real* world and live out the rest of his life in peace. It was evident to Adam that Mirror Lake was both a blessing and a curse.

When Lucci asked him if he'd consider remaining at Mirror Lake, Adam could not give him a definite answer. He loved the lake, and he never felt more alive. Yet, how could he be any better off than Lucci? What happiness would there be living alone, and not being able to tell anyone about this wonderful place? Now, that he was forty years younger, wouldn't it be better for *him* to return to the *real* world, and take full advantage of his second chance? He certainly wouldn't need an underwater cavern to be the nesting place of his *redeemed* life. Besides, being the guardian wasn't the same as being the one who was redeemed; unless of course, Adam Tiller *was* the chosen one. The only problem with this scenario is that it takes two, a male and a female, to start a new generation, and as of a few weeks ago there was no Mrs. Tiller in the picture!

Was Adam being too selfish? Shouldn't he be thinking of the human race? He could possibly one day be its only hope! One thing was certain; Adam wasn't ready to give Lucci his final answer. There was too much to flesh out in his mind. It was too significant a decision to take lightly, and without giving it ample thought. He needed additional time.

Lucci seemed satisfied with Adam's delay, and was relieved that he hadn't refused to at least consider the possibility. At the end of lunch Adam asked Lucci to give him a week or two at the most, so he could give the process the proper attention it warranted. Lucci agreed to his terms. Adam promised that he'd give him a call, once he arrived at a decision. After finishing their meal, Lucci thanked Adam, and after shaking hands, the once-guardian of Mirror Lake departed. Adam elected to clean up later having so much on his mind, and wanting to start thinking, now. *What better place to think than, here, at Mirror Lake? It has brought me this far, so why wouldn't it make it clear to me, just what I am supposed to do?*

He gathered the new array of healthy snacks and bottled water, as well as his fishing gear, and started out. It was another gorgeous day on the lake. The sky was blue and filled with large puffy cumulus clouds that provided a magnificent backdrop for Adam's mission. He sat in the boat for nearly an hour before he made a single cast. He would maintain the usual daily routine for as long as it was necessary, but would be more introspective when it came to his journal. He wanted to be in touch with his feelings, his inner soul, and hopefully with God Himself. He believed that God was the Creator of this paradise, but was it for the purpose that Lucci suggested? *Am I truly the chosen one? Am I half of the couple needed to redeem mankind? If I am, where is my mate?*

He aimed to be more attentive to how God may try to communicate with him. The walk in the woods, and time in the boat or on the porch would become opportunities to meet his Creator heart to heart. He recalled something his mother once said; *Prayer isn't a one way street. It requires us to listen, and not to always be the one doing the talking.* Adam never really listened to many people, let alone to God. Now, was as good a time as ever to start. Each time he'd think about his decision, Adam would set the pros and cons of saying either Yes or No. After he thought and prayed, Adam sat back, and gave God a chance to talk to him. Through this new prayer posture, he became more relaxed and felt an inner serenity than he had never before experienced. For the first time in his life, Adam could appreciate the people who practiced *Yoga*, as did his wife, and not poke fun at them. Like Yoga, prayer could result in peace of mind, body, and spirit; a quality of life in which one can never have enough or not have at all.

There was no doubt in Adam's mind, that the decision to stay or leave Mirror Lake wasn't going to be an easy one, yet he was determined to make it within the two weeks he promised. He set his watch alarm for two weeks from the time Lucci left the cabin. His plan was to think and pray every day for no more than an hour at a single setting. At the end of the hour, he'd stop and continue with whatever was part of his daily routine. He believed that people can think too much at times, making things only worse. He didn't want to push the issue, but rather, take it slowly, one day at a time.

While in the boat one afternoon, the alarm on his watch signaled the end of his period of discernment, and he was no closer to a decision than he was at the outset. He promised to call Lucci no later than in two weeks, but if he did today, he would have to tell him that he was at a stalemate. He stared into the lake, that at first made Adam see things about him that he didn't like, but after the plunge, allowed him to see the person that he could still become. *How could I become, if I have no opportunity to find out what I could be?*

If anything, he felt closer to making the decision to leave Mirror Lake than to stay, but he wasn't totally convinced that it was the best choice. He wondered if the lake had anything to reveal to him that would help him arrive at his decision. *Is it time for another plunge?* He was no longer afraid of becoming any younger, since Lucci assured him that it wasn't going to happen. However, he thought that if anything, the lake would beckon him to stay. He didn't want to be coerced, but preferred to make the choice freely, and after having thoroughly weighed both the pros and the cons.

It was decision time. He had thought and prayed long enough. *There are times in life that you sometimes have to stop thinking so much, and go where your heart takes you.* Adam took a deep breath, pulled up anchor, and started back to the cabin.

Chapter Fourteen

A Life Changing Decision

Although the two-week period of discernment had come to an end, Adam still wasn't absolutely certain what to do. He returned to the cabin, and called Lucci as he had promised. He told him that he was close to making the decision, but needed one more day. Lucci was willing to give him another day, or a second if necessary. Adam thanked the proprietor for his understanding and patience. After his conversation, Adam showered and prepared a light meal. He wrote a journal entry for the day that included his final arguments for and against leaving Mirror Lake. He went to bed hoping that the morning would bring him the answer for which he was seeking. After finishing *Moby Dick*, he turned on his side, and was asleep before he could rehash all the arguments and be up for half the night.

He rose early in the morning feeling refreshed, and saw on his iPhone that it was July 8th. It would have been his wife's sixty-third birthday. He thought that it may be a good omen. He fried eggs, home-fried potatoes, and had two slices of unbuttered toast with grapefruit juice. He chose not to brew another pot of coffee. After breakfast, he sat on the porch, and watched the loon chicks playing in the channel. He was amazed at how quickly they were growing. He threw bread crumbs between the dock and the cabin. His feathered-friends feasted on the treat, and ventured onto the porch to pick up the remaining crumbs that were only a couple of feet from Adam. He tried to get them to eat off his hand, but was unsuccessful. He had better luck with Storm, who arrived after the loons had made their way to the lake. Not only would the fawn eat off his hand, but she also allowed him to pet her. Adam Tiller was becoming a real Francis of Assisi, the thirteenth century friar known for his respect for nature and love of animals.

While he was taking his daily stroll through the woods, he marveled at how keen his senses had become. Upon his return to the lodge, he found the groceries left by Lucci on the porch, and put them away. He recalled meeting Lucci for the first time and was still amazed by his youthful appearance, yet not taken back as much as Peale and other people will be, once they'd lay eyes on the new Adam. For a moment he was filled with sadness as he thought of Lucci's son on his death bed, and the anguish that Lucci must be feeling. *No child should die before his parent.*

It was wonderful to be young again, but how could he ever explain his transformation to Peale, Mrs. Ritter, or to anyone else who knew him? This was the major negative aspect that tipped the balance in favor of remaining at

Mirror Lake. Even if people did believe him, telling the truth would reveal the secret, and if Lucci was right, the new world could possibly be exploited or defiled by the wrong people. He didn't want to be responsible for its demise, if it indeed was created by God to give mankind a second chance. He couldn't do it to Lucci either, especially while he was grieving the near-death of his son. He wasn't happy being in a position that forced him into making a decision. He would much rather choose freely the path to take. Undoubtedly, it was the most perplexing decision that had ever confronted him.

Whatever course he'd choose to take; his life would change drastically. Either decision would lead him into a world of uncertainty. If he chose to return to Manhattan, he'd have to explain his age regression without revealing the secret of Mirror Lake. If he chose to stay; who would be his partner? Perhaps replacing Lucci as the guardian of the secret was a compromise. It seemed the easiest path to take. All he had to do was to remain at the place that he had grown to love, and as Lucci had done; find a couple who would be the *first parents* of the redeemed human race. After a half hour of further reflection, he concluded that the only thing that could help him to make the choice was Mirror Lake. *Here, I go again. I feel as if I'm being tossed around like a ping pong ball! Why can't I make a definite decision to go one way or the other? I can't figure out where my mind OR heart is trying to take me.* He believed that the lake protected him in the fog, and had drastically altered him. Now, he believed that it would be his guide.

It was another beautiful day on the lake. The only blemish to the perfect weather throughout his stay at

Mirror Lake was the one storm that suddenly erupted, yet he wasn't sure if that was a flaw, as much as it was nature's way of expressing itself. The sky was painted with the most stunning shade of blue, and the clouds seemed to tower for miles into the heavens. The loons and other aquatic animals seemed more abundant than ever. He was entertained by the diving birds that easily plucked one fish after another from the lake. He could share the joy of the birds; having fished with equal success every day or night that he cast his line into the enchanted body of water.

As he rowed across the lake closer to the shore, he spied a beaver busily constructing a dam across a channel similar to the one where the cabin stood. He stopped for a moment to watch the creature that didn't seem to notice the voyeur, or perhaps really didn't care. There was no doubt in his mind that the wildlife of Mirror Lake was different. Not only were the animals healthier, larger and more colorful, but they were also less fearful of man. There seemed to be a harmony among all life on the lake; a quality that did not exist in Adam's world. He now believed that had the black bear seen him at the side of the cabin, it would have ignored him and continued to rummage through the trash cans. However, he wasn't ready to test his hypothesis! He was convinced that the entire lake was paradise; not only its subterranean region and that its water was responsible for the miraculous effect on all the life connected to it.

He conjectured that this effect was evident on the flora of the area as well. He thought that compared to the day he arrived at Mirror Lake, the trees and shrubs were now taller, greener and plusher. There was certainly an intimate and powerful link between all life on the lake. He too, was starting to feel a similar connection with the lake, its life, and surroundings.

The pensive boater moved on, until he arrived to the part of the lake where he figured would be the underwater cavern, the portal to the *redeemed world*, as spoken by Lucci. He hoped that his enchanting escort would surface, and gesture him to follow her. He stopped rowing and relaxed. He took out a bag of trail mix to nibble on, and was attentive to the sights and sounds of the lake. Without any introduction, a large bird resembling an albatross flew on the bow of the boat facing him. It was beige in color with black lines on its underbelly. It had a bright orange beak, larger than the gulls he'd seen on the beach. As the bird opened its wings to Adam's surprise, he saw a vast array of colored-stripes on the inside. He didn't believe that any bird of this kind existed outside the confines of Mirror Lake. He laughed, half-expecting the creature to begin talking to him. It wouldn't be a shock; given what he had experienced over the last few weeks.

He grabbed a small handful of trail mix, and held out his hand hoping that his feathered-friend would take it. What happened next blew Adam's mind. The bird began to flap its wings, and slowly rose from the bow more like a hummingbird than a gull. It hovered over the palm of his hand, and proceeded to eat off it with no inhibition. After it cleaned off Adam's hand, the bird flew backwards, and returned to its perch. Adam filled his hand with more food, and once again held it out. Having enjoyed the treat, the bird once again approached its feeder, and ate all of the trail mix. After repeating the gesture one more time, apparently the creature had enough. As it flew backwards, it hovered in the air for a brief moment, and finally darted away. It was an exquisite performance that almost prompted Adam to give it a standing ovation!

Why would I ever want to leave this enchanted place? Adam had a notion that all he had seen was only a small token of the lake's complete treasure. How exciting would it be, to spend more months discovering all that it had to offer? However, the hands of time had been turned back for him. Conceivably, God's plan could have been to give *him* a second chance, so now, he could return home to do the things that he should have done the first time around. Isn't this the way things work? The events that occur in one's life can be viewed in a variety of ways. The same event experienced by two different people can take on two totally different meanings; depending on how the event is interpreted. Coming to Mirror Lake could have been for Adam's benefit, and no one else's. Yet, how could he be certain? It was at this point that Adam knew the only way to arrive at this certainty was to take the plunge. The lake itself would, indeed, provide him with an answer.

He couldn't understand why he was so apprehensive in returning to the underwater paradise. He knew that it wouldn't cause any more age regression; perhaps it was because he didn't want it to sway him to stay. He realized that he couldn't make the decision on his own, and plausibly needed to be swayed in one direction or another. *Am I destined to have come to this amazing place for a short time, change, and then, return to my former world having been given a second chance? Or, is it my destiny to learn about its secret, change, and then, become a part of it?* He had dug as deeply within himself as possible, and was at a stalemate.

It was time to stop thinking, and allow the lake to show him the path that he should take.

He pulled up the oars and started to row back, since he had drifted away from the section of the lake where he imagined the portal would be. It was a hot July afternoon, and despite his dark tan, he could still feel the hot rays of the sun on his shoulders and the top of his head. The temperature on the lake was easily ninety degrees Fahrenheit, if not closer to the century mark. It was more reason to take a dip, and once in the water to return to his new world. Unfortunately, he had been thinking too much, so had forgotten to wear his swim suit under his shorts. It really wouldn't matter. He didn't think that the fish would care. Hoping that Ariel wouldn't be waiting for him once he broke the surface of the water, Adam Tiller did something that he had never done before. He swam in the nude.

After a brief swim, that didn't take him more than fifty feet from the boat, he returned and climbed back into it. He was glad that he had taken a dip for it was extremely refreshing; however the thought of swimming to the cavern in the buff prevented him from trying to find it. He dried off, and slipped into his shorts. He finished off the bag of trail mix and after downing a second bottle of water, chose to return to the cabin. It wasn't wearing his birthday suit that prompted the move, but a strong feeling that had come over him during the swim. Maybe the lake did provide the answer without Adam having to go into the cavern one more time.

As he rowed back to the shanty, Adam looked with great satisfaction at the muscles that he had developed in both his arms and legs. He glided swiftly across the lake exhausting little energy, and without any pain. His body was well-toned, lungs as clean as a whistle, and his five senses never keener. His mind was as sharp as a tack. He had become a different man, a better one; possessing a new resolve and purpose in life. If he could look into himself and see his soul, Adam was certain that it, too, had become a new creation.

He showered upon his return, and sat on the porch with his laptop. He recorded his experience with the exotic bird and reflected deeply about the feeling that had overcome him during the swim. At the end of the entry he typed these words.

> . . . *Thus, I have decided to leave my beautiful paradise; not to return to my former way of life, but to make my final decision. I have come to the conclusion that a decision can not be made here. Now, all I must do is to arrive at an explanation of how a sixty-three year old has become a man forty years younger!*

Adam thought more about it during and after dinner, but came up with no better choice. It wasn't every day that such a story made the headlines of the local or national newspapers. As he passed the bookcase on the way to the kitchen, he spied a book that contained a collection of short stories written by F. Scott Fitzgerald. He remembered one he read in college that had intrigued him, so looked to see if it was there. The work was not as well-known as some of his others such as *The Great Gatsby*, yet it still had a fascinating story line. It was entitled *The Curious Case of Benjamin Button*. The tale was about a man who had a rare disease in which he was born as an old man, but grew into a younger one; not so far removed from his own situation. He was delighted to have found it, and immediately sat on the recliner to read it.

Adam was more fascinated by the story this time around; having read it in the context of his own situation. As he thought more about arriving at an explanation for his age regression upon his return home, he was drawn to the Bible which was also part of the collection of books on the bookcase. He was particularly interested in reading the first few chapters of the Book of Genesis that contained the story of the creation of man and woman. For the first time in his life, he made a connection with Adam, the first man created by God, but what struck him the most was to read that Adam was a "tiller" of the land. Was it a coincidence that his name was "Adam Tiller," or was it a connection? As he read further into the Book of Genesis, he learned that in addition to Cain and Abel, Adam also had another son named Seth. He returned the Bible to the bookcase, and sat on the recliner grinning from ear to ear. He wasn't certain if he should give God or himself the credit, but he had just come up with the perfect explanation.

Chapter Fifteen

Meet Seth Tiller

*A*dam didn't sleep for more than a few hours, and awoke still excited about his plan. While he was eating breakfast, he was startled by a rap on the door. When he opened it, he saw a somber-looking Lucci. Adam welcomed him, and invited Lucci to join him for breakfast. The man didn't have very good news to share. His son took a sudden turn for the worse a week ago, and died on the Fourth of July. This saddened Adam, but Lucci was glad that it was over. He thought it was appropriate that his son, a veteran of the Viet Nam War, left this world on the national celebration of Independence Day, for he was, now, free from his suffering and pain. Lucci himself was set free from the years of pain, watching his son grow old and sickly, as he remained young and robust.

Adam extended his most sincere condolences, and asked if he wanted to stay with him in the cabin. He suggested that a little fishing on Mirror Lake would help him to deal with the grief of losing his son. Adam was sure that Lucci was well aware of the healing power of the lake. Lucci was very grateful, accepted his offer, but said that he wouldn't stay for very long. All he wanted to do was to spend a couple of hours on the lake, and didn't have to do any fishing. It didn't surprise Adam that Lucci took a swimsuit, and a change of clothes. Before Lucci set out, Adam invited him to stay for lunch or dinner, depending on the time he'd return from the lake. There was no hurry for him to leave, and Adam knew that spending time on the lake would be his best medicine.

Adam wanted to maintain his daily routine, so prepared to set out for his walk in the woods. He penned a brief note telling Lucci where he'd be, invited him again to stay for a meal, and to remain overnight if he so desired. He also added that he had arrived at his decision. If anything, this last line would keep Lucci from wanting to leave without at least seeing Adam.

It was another hot day at Mirror Lake, but the woods made it feel much cooler. Adam seemed to have enjoyed his adventure more today, than on other days. He was sure that it was because he had finally made his decision. On the way back to the hovel, Adam considered doing something that he hadn't done in over fifty years, namely, to climb a tree. This desire had to be the result of his age regression for he'd never have entertained such a crazy idea a month ago. He looked up a tall pine tree, and saw that it had low strong branches. He started to giggle, and felt quite giddy. *What has come over me?* After pausing for a few seconds, he chose to go for it. He marveled how easily he ascended the tree. He used muscles in his arms and legs, that hadn't stretched in decades. As he reached the acme of his climb, he recalled the words of his old Scoutmaster, *Whatever you do, boy, don't look down!* He didn't heed the warning then, nor was he going to do it now. Even though he was twenty-three, he still had the same feeling as a boy of twelve, and it wasn't a good one.

While he sat perched in the tree that had to be at least forty feet from the ground, and calculating how he was going to get down, he noticed a bird's nest a few feet away. Nestled inside, were five fledglings with their beaks wide open, and crying out in hunger.

I suppose they think that I'm their mother? This thought was followed by a more frightening one. *What if the real mama bird comes back?* Trying not to panic and imagining himself being pecked to death by the mother, he started to feel for a lower branch without looking down. Having found one, he began to descend and slowly made his way to safe ground. He breathed a sigh of relief, wiped his brow as he looked up, and saw a large bird that resembled a hawk flying to the nest. He had escaped in the nick of time. If he hadn't learned a lesson as a Boy Scout, he certainly learned it today. He'd never climb a tree again, no matter how young or bold he imagined himself to be!

When he returned to the lodge, he saw that the boat was moored, and that Lucci was showering. Adam was glad that Lucci had elected to stay at least long enough to hear him out. The two men sat on the porch sipping on iced tea. Lucci didn't say anything about what he did on the lake, but Adam told him of his tree-climbing adventure that made Lucci laugh hysterically. Adam could see that the lake had a healing effect on him.

Adam learned two things about himself during their dialogue, first; that he could tell a funny story, and second; that he could actually hold a decent conversation with another human being. He wasn't very good at either for most of his adult life, but now, found both to be easy and enjoyable.

Lucci spoke about the marriage to his wife, Concetta, the joy of being a father, as well as the sadness of losing both of them. He felt that they were cheated from the gift that he had been given through no merit of his own, yet in spite of his sadness at their loss, confessed that he would do it all over again for he had lived a full and happy life.

In a way Adam envied him, but also it made a solid case for leaving Mirror Lake. Despite an inkling of apprehension, it was time to reveal his decision. Lucci listened attentively, asked no questions, nor made any comments. After Adam finished telling him his plan upon his return to Manhattan, Lucci told him that he liked it and believed that it could possibly work. The two men, now friends, enjoyed a delicious dinner, and sat at the kitchen table for two hours talking about a number of things. Lucci graciously accepted Adam's decision, as well as his departure from Mirror Lake before his four month lease ran out. Adam insisted that he keep the money even though he wouldn't be using the cabin for the remaining time on the lease agreement. It wasn't about the money, but what Adam must now set out to do. Reluctantly, Lucci agreed to Adam's terms, and the two men shook hands. He wished Adam well before leaving, and started out while there was still light.

After Adam cleaned up, he took out his laptop and at the kitchen table initiated the first step of his plan-an e-mail to his publisher, Vincent Peale. He chuckled as he began to type.

My dear Vincent,

During my stay in the northwoods, a most exciting, and life-changing event took place. As I was doing some research for my new book, I received a most unusual e-mail from a young man by the name of Seth Tiller. I thought at first, that he might have been a distant relative. He had a remarkable story, so remarkable, that I flew him out to my cabin.

Vincent, I have a son, as hard as it is to believe! I am sending him to join you in a few days. I want you to set him up in my apartment, and give him a grand tour of the publishing house. He, too, is a writer and we may very well offer him a position with the company. I have never been happier in my life!

I will remain here to finish my novel, which I might add is coming along very well, and will be a sure best seller. Perhaps my best ever! I am certain that you are going to like Seth. You'll agree that he is a real "chip off the old block!"

Sincerely,

Adam

As he hit the send button, a huge grin traveled across his face reaching from ear to ear. He closed his laptop, and cried in jubilation, "I have a son!" He looked at the loon clock and saw that he had time to view the setting of the sun, so he hurried to fetch a few things and started out for the lake.

Rowing onto the lake on this special night left Adam with a different feeling, as if he was a young boy approaching his dad with something exciting to tell him. He likened it to chatting with his dad about getting his favorite baseball player's trading card in an old wax pack. This time, it wouldn't be his father with whom to share his excitement, but Mirror Lake. When he arrived at the middle of the lake, he stopped rowing and sat talking to the lake, while the sky was performing its spectacular color show. If someone was watching, he'd think that Adam was crazy. It was the magic of the lake that had taken over him. He imagined Lucci having done the same thing earlier in the day. Mirror Lake was now, more a person, than a body of water. He felt as if he owed it for his new beginning, and second chance in life.

As nature's fireworks came to an end and the dark blue of the sky was now taking over, Adam could no longer hold back his emotions and started to cry. It was as if he was mourning the death of his own self, yet shedding tears of joy for his new one. He felt cleansed by the healing waters of Mirror Lake, and felt as if he was truly "born again." He humbled himself before God, thanking Him for the opportunity to start anew, and promised that this time; he'd do things right.

He rowed back to his hovel, and called the airlines hoping to book a flight to New York as soon as possible. He'd have to settle for a flight in three days, but there was always a chance of a cancellation. He showered, and ate leftovers from the meal with Lucci. He relaxed on the sofa, and imagined life as Seth Tiller. He hadn't totally ruled out returning to Mirror Lake, as he told Lucci. Just as he had felt the lake calling to him during his stay, he now heard a different calling. He knew that he had to return to the Big Apple for just as his senses, instincts, and intellect had grown sharper, so had his intuition. He had no doubt in his mind that he would find out something far greater than an answer to his dilemma. In New York City, he would discover the true meaning of his life, and his ultimate destiny.

Chapter Sixteen

The Departure of Adam Tiller

A dam fell asleep on the sofa, and at seven-thirty he was awakened by the ringing of his cell phone. It was a representative from the airlines. He was delighted to learn that someone canceled, giving Adam a ticket for an evening flight. As he hit the end button, the reality of the situation set in. He had spent forty days at Mirror Lake, and there was a possibility that he might never return. He ate a quick breakfast, and then called Lucci asking if he could drive him to the airport. Lucci was pleased to do him the favor, and the rendezvous was set at seven p.m. on the road where he had been dropped off by the taxi.

There wasn't much to pack, and any groceries would be used by Lucci. Adam had the rest of the day before leaving Mirror Lake, so chose to take his usual walk in the woods, and spend a few hours fishing. He didn't venture too far from the cabin, and he shortened the hike considerably. He preferred to spend most of the time on the lake. As the skiff made its way to the main body of the lake, he noticed that the sky was overcast for the first time since the storm. Adam imagined that it was the lake's response to his departure. He rowed to where he believed the underwater cavern would be and stopped. He pulled in the oars, and reflected on the experience at this special place. All that had happened still remained a mystery in part, yet he felt that it was for a reason.

After awhile, his thoughts moved from the past to the future. If he chose to stay in Manhattan to start a new life as Seth Tiller, he had to decide what he was going to do with Adam Tiller. He sat for almost an hour contemplating ways to plan his sudden disappearance. Perhaps he could chose to have Adam reside permanently at Mirror Lake, and still write for Peale. Maybe he could orchestrate his accidental death, which Lucci would help him to implement. He imagined how his obituary might read.

. . . Funeral arrangements were made by Mister Michael Lucci, who was given the power of attorney. He honored Mr. Tiller's request to have a private funeral, and be laid to rest in an unmarked grave on the land that he had come to love. Mister Tiller is survived by his son, Seth Tiller, who inherited the popular writer's entire fortune . . .

He would also arrange that Peale would be taken good care of financially by giving him his share of the publishing house and a nice chunk of money for his many years of service. Tiller knew him all too well. The handsome settlement would prevent Peale from asking questions, and especially from being suspicious of Seth.

Adam's thoughts returned to Mirror Lake. There was a part of him that wanted to stay. Unlike Lucci, who had a wife and son, Tiller had no one. He could easily choose to stay for he loved the lake, and felt an intimate connection to it. Besides, he could always take the plunge, and learn more about its secret. On the other hand, there was something that he wasn't clearly seeing here. Somehow, the missing piece would be discovered upon his return to the city. If the answer wasn't to be found in Manhattan, he'd come back to the lake, and as Lucci had suggested, learn to accept the mystery and become more comfortable not knowing all the answers. He had to at least make the effort. Better to have tried now, than to have future regrets.

Not wanting to over-analyze and change his mind again, he began to fish. As always, he pulled in the usual abundant catch. He thought about Ariel and Aunt Bea, wondering if they'd know of his planned departure, and make one last appearance. It began to rain, as if the lake was mourning its loss. It didn't deter him from fishing, although it was as good time as ever to change his position. He rowed along the bank, and passed the beaver that was still working diligently on its fortification. He was entertained once again, by the diving birds that were enjoying another food fest. Life on Mirror Lake would still continue in Adam's absence, yet perhaps hoping for his return one day.

When he found a suitable spot to fish, he opted for a bite to eat before he'd cast another line. Adam was certain of one thing, namely, that he was going to miss the peace and quiet that the lake had provided. Returning to New York meant a return to the *rat race*, to the noise and distractions of life, the hustle and bustle, deadlines, and all the things that Adam had forgotten about and didn't miss one bit. Once again, he had to redirect his thoughts for he didn't want to think his way out of leaving. He didn't entertain the notion of taking a swim in fear that he might see Ariel, and be lured to the underwater paradise. After finishing his snack, he chose not to fish anymore, and began to make his way to the cabin. As he neared the channel, he halted for a brief moment, and as he stood in the boat, took in the lake for conceivably the final time. A tear came to his eye as he whispered, "Good-bye my love, and thank you."

He docked the vessel more securely than usual, rinsed off the fishing equipment, and returned it to the shed. He released the night crawlers from the carton, and watched them inch across the land, enjoying their new-found freedom. He locked the sheds, covered the pile of cedar logs with a tarp, and tied it down. He tidied the inside of the cabin and showered. He packed his suitcase and carry-on, and then enjoyed an early-evening dinner. He sat on the recliner to write the final entry of his amazing account of life at Mirror Lake. He didn't have an adequate amount of material for a full-length novel, but knew that his forty day stay would provide a good start. There would be more to write, perhaps the most significant of all. At six-thirty, he gathered his belongings, and headed out for the one mile walk to his rendezvous with Lucci. As he was about to lock the front door, and place the key under the mat, he remembered that he had one more chore to perform. He left some fruit on the porch for Storm, and spread a couple slices of bread along the bank of the channel for the loon family. He even left a pile of pretzels should the raccoon return. As for as Baby Bear, well, he was on his own.

He grabbed his bags and started out for the highway. When Adam arrived, he saw that Lucci was parked on the side of the road. During the drive to the airport, Adam thanked the proprietor for all he had done to make his stay at Mirror Lake, a delightful one. Lucci revealed that the cabin as well as the lake and its surroundings, were given to him by the previous guardian. It made sense, for how else could Lucci had prevented anyone from building close to the cabin? The lake hadn't belonged to any individual outside of the loop for as long as Lucci knew. It was the reason why it's secret could have been protected for centuries. Lucci tried to persuade Adam to accept a refund since he wasn't staying for the remaining term on his lease, but he still refused. Lucci insisted that the money didn't matter as much as the freedom he'd enjoy, if only someone was willing to replace him as the lake's guardian. In Adam's mind he knew that there was a possibility that he'd return one day to fulfill Lucci's dream, but he had to let whatever was going to occur in Manhattan come to be. Lucci expressed his best wishes, and hoped that Adam would find for what he was searching. He also told the writer that he wouldn't harbor any ill-feelings should he choose not to return. He appreciated the fact that Tiller was given a second chance in life, and was not about to begrudge him for wanting to be happy.

When the men reached the airport, they hugged outside of the car, and Adam made his way to the plane terminal. He checked in his baggage, and boarded the airplane with no glitch. For the time being, he had to forget Mirror Lake, and focus on his new life. He closed his eyes as the plane took off, and rehearsed what he was going to say to Peale. He had to be careful about what he'd say, and how he'd say it, as well as to refrain from any particular words, phrases, or mannerisms that would heighten the publisher's suspicion.

There weren't any photographs lying around of Adam's youth. There were no high school or college yearbooks, so he wasn't worried about Peale falling upon any evidence that would stir his curiosity. Not only would he find an uncanny resemblance between Seth and his father, he'd also have to conclude that Seth is a dead ringer! Even if Peale was suspicious of Seth, would he believe for a single moment that this twenty-three year old could possibly be Adam Tiller? Adam was convinced that it wasn't going to happen. He had contrived a masterful explanation for Seth's existence. Peale was going to accept it, so there was no sweat off Adam's brow.

There was a brief delay at the airport in Green Bay, due to a severe thunderstorm that was passing. Adam sat in the terminal next to a family that included three small children. One of the little boys that he figured was about four, kept staring at Adam, making him feel uncomfortable. The kid approached him, and asked his name. He smiled at the boy, and replied that it was "Adam." He instantly realized his mistake, and reminded himself that he had to be more careful. It was the sort of slip up that would be devastating if made in front of Peale. On the opposite side of the seating area were two young girls entertaining themselves with a memory game. For forty days, he hadn't heard the sound of children at play. Normally, he'd get up, and search for a quieter place to sit for he didn't like being around kids. Today was different. He actually enjoyed listening to their cheerful voices. He truly was a changed man.

Chapter Seventeen

The Arrival of Seth Tiller

Seth walked to the front desk of his high rise complex on Fifth Avenue and Fifty-Eighth Street. As *Adam Tiller*, he had called the desk to inform the concierge that his son was coming, and to give him a spare key. His condo was on the twenty-first floor, and it overlooked Central Park. When Seth walked in, he could hardly recognize it; thanks to Peale who had immediately hired a maid service to give it a thorough dusting and cleaning.

He really didn't miss his apartment, the big city, his work, or life in general. He was already missing Mirror Lake, and part of him wished that he had never left. The other part of him knew that there was a definite purpose for his return, and that only time would tell. He hoped that it would take the shortest amount time. He placed his clothing in the hamper, and would give them a good washing in the morning. He showered, put on a set of casuals, and headed out to a local pizzeria for a bite to eat. Funny how quickly he returned to the old habit of eating out. He was well aware of this, and vowed that it was only for his first night at home. He was dead set against picking up the far worse bad habits of excessive drinking and smoking. In fact he now had a zero tolerance for both.

When he returned to his pad, he looked at the bar, and for a moment thought of how good a dry martini would taste right now. He was able to resist the temptation and was proud of himself as he passed the bar, and walked into the kitchen. Peale hadn't been as accommodating as Lucci, for there was nothing fresh waiting for him in the fridge or the food pantry. It was too late to go shopping, so he planned to go in the morning after doing something that he hadn't done in years—attend Sunday Mass at Saint Patrick's Cathedral.

He couldn't recall the last time he attended services there, other than for his wife's funeral a month and a half ago. He thought that he owed God, who Adam felt was behind the miracle on Mirror Lake, a visit, and could be directing his actions. The cathedral was less than a mile away, and although he would have driven there in the past, chose to go by foot tomorrow. In this way he'd at least keep up with his daily walk. It would be quite a different stroll, but nonetheless, it would at least be a form of exercise.

He also planned to visit his publishing house that was located in lower Manhattan, a few blocks from the memorial of the World Trade Center. He would be meeting Peale for the first time, and he wasn't looking forward to it. Seth wasn't tired, so chose to take a walk in Central Park. It was a far cry from the peace and quiet of Wisconsin's northwoods, yet it was all the woods that he had in his immediate area.

It was extremely hot and humid in the city, unlike to what he was accustomed at Mirror Lake. He strolled thoughtlessly for a few blocks, and sat alone on a bench. It was easier to concentrate on the lake for there were too many distractions in Central Park, even in the early morning hours. There were a considerable number of people in the park trying to keep cool. He had grown fond of the silence in the wilderness, hearing only the scurrying of animals and buzzing of insects, the wind blowing through the trees, fish jumping in and out of the water, and rain tapping on the roof of the log cabin. Now, these sounds were replaced by idle chatter, the laughs and screams of people, the honking horns, and blaring of sirens. With his sharpened senses it seemed that Adam could hear just about everything, however he couldn't hear a single voice or groan coming from within him.

He returned to his apartment without any new revelation, but feeling hot, irritable, and sticky. He wasn't off to a good start, but told himself that he had to be patient. Ah, yes, patience! It is a virtue that he lacked throughout his entire life. He elected to jump into the shower, and had to admit that it was nice taking a hot shower for a change. He grabbed a bottle of Perrier from the fridge, and plopped on his plush leather sofa to watch a rebroadcast of the eleven o'clock news. There wasn't much different from the last time he watched the news. There were the usual shootings, robberies, drug raids, and all the other things that went with summer in the city. He was lifted up a bit when he saw that the Phillies defeated the

Mets at Citizen's Bank Park by the score of 4 to 1. The Phils won a string of division championships, but had come upon some bad times of late. Even though they were in last place tied with the Marlins, Adam didn't give up hope for their resurgence as one of Baseball's finest.

He wasn't sure of the Mass schedule at Saint Pat's, so he went on the Internet to check out the website. Given the time that he'd be heading to bed, he opted for the noon Mass. He also went on his own website that is operated by Peale. In addition to the usual posts and blogs, there was a blurb that promised a "new and riveting" novel by Adam Tiller, soon to be released. Was Peale in for a rude awakening!

He peered into the corner of the living room where there was a cardboard box filled with mail. He had no desire to go through any of it, so turned off his HD plasma television, and made his way to the bedroom. Wanting to keep up with his newly-established *good* habit of reading before going to bed, he looked on his bookcase for an appealing book. Nothing stood out to him. He spied a pile of books that must have been put aside by Marie for her book club, but never were able to read due to her illness. He picked up a few that he concluded were definite No's, and then saw one that may have some promise. It was entitled *The Lucky One*, written by the popular romance writer, Nicholas Sparks, who Adam met a number of times, and had found to be quite delightful.

Tiller wasn't particularly fond of romance novels, and wouldn't normally think of reading one; however, he was a changed man, and wasn't going to rule out a little romance in his new life. Besides, he was intrigued by the title, and felt a bit lucky himself. He took the book, and sat on the recliner, so to gaze at the artificial fireplace hoping to duplicate the ambiance found in the cabin on Mirror Lake. He brought the thermostat down to compensate for the heat that would be emitted by the fire. It was a huge disappointment to Adam, for the gas-burning fireplace didn't come close to the real thing. He missed the colorful dancing of flames from one log to another, the crackling sound of the wood, and the sweet aroma of burning cedar.

Before he opened the book he remembered that he hadn't entered a journal entry for the day, so he retrieved his laptop, and returned to the sofa. He thought about his departure from Mirror Lake, his flight, and stroll in Central Park. Compared to what he grew accustomed to writing, he had very little to add, in fact, there was nothing exciting to be worthy of a chapter in his new book. He ended up writing the shortest of all the entries that he had composed in the last forty days. When he finished, he laid the laptop on the floor, picked up the novel, and sank into the recliner. He didn't get passed the first few pages when he started to nod. Within minutes he was sound asleep. The length of the day filled with mixed emotions was too much for even a young man of twenty-three to take.

He woke up in the middle of the night, and turned off the fireplace. For a moment he thought of sleeping in bed, but didn't want to ruffle the blanket and sheets for just a few more hours of sleep. He remained in the living room, but shifted from the recliner to the sofa, where he was able to lie more comfortably.

He looked around in the room, and compared it to the one in the cabin. He visualized where the raccoon, buck, and black bear would be. He also recalled the porch on which he'd sit for hours, taking in the cool fresh air, feeding Storm, and watching the loons play gleefully in the channel. There was no consolation returning to Manhattan. He pined for the place that had given back his life, and wondered if that was where he should be. He could appreciate the old adage; "Absence makes the heart grow fonder," even when related to places, and not particularly to people. He realized that he hadn't given himself enough time, having only been home for a few hours. He had to be more patient. He'd feel better in the morning after a few hours of sleep, and would awake to a new day full of possibilities.

The feeling of emptiness that he was experiencing was similar to how he felt when his first novel was rejected by a publisher. He was so dejected that he was ready to give up writing, and seek another profession. If it wasn't for his future wife, he'd never have picked up the pen again. *Ah, those were the days. What ever happened to them?* It was too soon to throw in the towel. *Maybe God is leaving it up to me to open my own window or door, instead of waiting for one to open on its own. But, what could I possibly do?*

His strong inclination to think things out must have awakened him before he had slept a single hour. Once he was up, he couldn't fall back to sleep for the gears in his head were spinning uncontrollably. *Perhaps the door I could create is in the form of the new book that I promised to Peale.* He revisited his journal and starting from "Day One," skimmed through the entries. There were some he read more carefully than others, such as the ones concerning Ariel, Aunt Bea, and the underwater world.

After two hours of reading, and adding more description to the accounts, he needed a break. He stretched for a minute, and then went to the kitchen for another bottle of mineral water. He was itching to start writing a manuscript for his new book. After thinking it over at the sink, he made his way to the home office, where he sat in front of his personal computer. He paused for a moment to think of how he should begin. The title of the book would be a good start, even though it was usually the last thing he'd write. At times, he'd leave it to Peale to choose a title, but this time, it was as clear as the most beautiful day on Mirror Lake. He typed the cover sheet that included the title of his new book—*The Last Guardian*. When he added his name at the bottom of the page, a door had just been opened. At that very moment, Seth Tiller had officially entered the world of writing.

Knowing the importance of the first chapter of a work of fiction, he carefully crafted an opening that would hook the reader, and keep him or her from putting down the book. He was extremely satisfied with his product, and thought that he had written enough for the night. He was, now, tired, and chose to sleep in his bed after all. As he lay in bed, knowing that the sun would soon be peeking into his window, he said a brief prayer; asking God to make clear the path that he was to take in life.

Chapter Eighteen

The Pieces Start Coming Together

When the alarm of his digital clock sounded, Seth pushed the snooze button, turned on his other side, and slept for another half hour. Unlike his desire to rise and shine as he did at Mirror Lake full of energy and excitement, he would rather have slept for the rest of the morning. He wasn't as eager returning to the humdrum way of life before his experience in the northwoods of Wisconsin. He finally forced himself out of bed and needing to be shaken out of his malaise, decided to take a cold shower. He half-expected to see the face of a sixty-three year old man when he looked into the mirror, so was delighted when he noticed that there was no physical change. *It wasn't a bad dream after all. I am still Seth Tiller.*

He rummaged through his entire wardrobe looking for something a young man would wear to church, and found it difficult to find something that fit. His new well-toned physique that resulted from all the exercise over the last forty days did not make it an easy endeavor. At last, he found an old green golf shirt, and a pair of khakis that he'd feel comfortable wearing. He had to press the fold out of his slacks, and while he was at it, ironed his shirt, too. Finding a pair of underwear that still fit wasn't an easy chore, but slipping into a pair of socks, and old Dockers, weren't as hard. *At least my feet haven't shrunk like the rest of me!*

Seth started out early enough, so he could stop at a café en route to Saint Patrick's for a bagel and glass of orange juice. He was proud that he passed up the tall cup of flavored coffee and chocolate chip muffin that was a usual Sunday ritual. It was a beautiful morning to stroll along Fifth Avenue. It wasn't as hot and humid as last night. There was also a slight breeze that reminded Seth of walking through the woods at Mirror Lake. He was a half hour early for Mass, so made his way to a side altar in honor of the Blessed Virgin Mary. He lit a candle, as his mother used to do, and knelt to say a prayer. Seth couldn't remember the last time he implored Mary's intercession, but needing to pull out all stops, he felt compelled to ask her for help.

He noticed that there was a young woman about his age, also lighting a candle. She smiled at him, as she passed on the way back to her pew. She was the most beautiful woman he had ever seen. She was dressed in a modest blue dress that fit perfectly on her lean body. Her skin was olive in color, her hair a shiny brown that lay softly on her shoulders, and she had brown expressive eyes, as big as saucers. She was the closest woman that he had ever seen to a young Sophia Loren, who he had idolized as a boy. He thought for a moment, that perhaps being in the wilderness for such a long time, had left him ogling at the first woman he'd lay eyes on, but when he looked over to her again, he knew that she was indeed, a real knockout!

A sense of guilt came over him for thinking this way in church, so turned back to continue his prayer to the Virgin Mary. When he finished, he walked by the woman and as she looked at him, Seth returned her smile with one of his own. He strategically sat two rows behind the woman, so he could continue to keep her in his sight. As if she was as attracted to him, as he was to her, she looked back at Seth, and smiled again.

The young writer scanned the cathedral, and was impressed by the number of people that had gathered as it approached noon. He heard a bell ring, and from the back, a procession started up the center aisle led by a teenage boy carrying a cross, and flanked by two younger girls carrying lit candles. All three altar servers were wearing long beige robes with a leather necklace on which was attached a wooden cross. An older man holding the Book of Sacred Scripture or Lectionary followed the trio, and behind him walked four men and women, who would serve as Ministers of the Eucharist. An older priest wearing green vestments and favoring his right leg was the last person in the procession. Seth recognized him as the celebrant at his wife's funeral. A woman standing behind an ambo in the sanctuary led the congregation in the singing of the hymn *Praise to the Lord, the Almighty* as the majestic organ piped the tune that Seth remembered as a young boy. The

Catholic Church celebrated its liturgy with pomp, yet also with great reverence. The ritual of the Mass hadn't change very much over the centuries, and still gave those who were part of its celebration a sense of other-worldliness.

Seth listened attentively to the readings from the Bible, hoping that he'd glean something that would have special meaning for him. The man he had seen holding the Lectionary in the Entrance Procession walked behind a lectern, and began to proclaim a reading from the Book of Genesis, the first book of the Bible. Seth was astonished as he heard the same passage he read at Mirror Lake. Was it a coincidence or a connection? Its message intrigued him, and would remain with him for the remainder of the day.

> *The Lord God formed man out of the clay of the ground and blew into his nostrils the breath of life. He planted a Garden of Eden in the east and he placed there the man whom he had formed to cultivate and care for it. The Lord God said: 'It is not good for the man to be alone. I will make a suitable partner for him.' So the Lord God cast a deep sleep on the man, and while he was asleep, he took out one of his ribs and closed up its place with flesh. The Lord God then built up into a woman the rib that he had taken from the man. When he brought her to the man, the man said: 'This one at last, is bone of my bones and flesh of my flesh; this one shall be called Eve for out of man, this one was taken.' That is why a man leaves his father and mother and clings to his wife, and the two become one body.*

After Mass Seth watched as the young woman left the pew and proceeded to kneel on the altar rail in front of the tabernacle, a golden box where leftover hosts consecrated at Mass are reserved for private adoration. He rose from his seat, and sat in the first pew directly behind her. He was determined to engage her in conversation; something Adam Tiller would never have done. She rose from the altar rail and as she turned caught sight of Seth. He stood up and made her stop dead in her tracks. She asked if she knew him. He told her that he was new to the area. Knowing that it would be more respectful to talk outside rather than inside of the cathedral, the couple left and continued their dialogue in front of Saint Patrick's.

Seth felt very comfortable talking to the woman, as she seemed to be in talking to him. He didn't feel as if he'd be imposing on her privacy, when he asked if she came to church to ask God for something. She wasn't at all offended by his question, and confirmed that it was the very reason for which she had been attending Mass over the last two months. She admitted that she didn't attend church regularly, so Seth wasn't embarrassed confessing that neither did he.

The woman directed the conversation to Seth, and asked why he had returned to church. He explained that he was seeking God's help in making an important career decision. He wondered if she would rather have heard him say, *to meet the right woman*. Seth didn't want their conversation to end, so to avoid going their separate ways and never to see each other again, he invited her to lunch with him. Without hesitation, she accepted his offer, and the two began to walk up the avenue in lively conversation toward the café where Seth had eaten a couple of hours ago.

It was an absolutely gorgeous summer afternoon, so the couple chose to sit outside at a small wrought-iron table topped by an umbrella. Seth was captivated by the woman's beauty, her expressive eyes, and vibrant personality. She was the type of person that you meet for the first time, yet think that you've known for your entire life. She told Seth that she was living with a friend she met at NYC, and that she graduated in May with a degree in Marketing. She had a summer internship with Merrill Lynch, and was planning to return to Narberth, Pennsylvania, once it was completed; unless of course, she was fortunate to be offered a job there. If offered a job, she'd move somewhere in North Jersey where it would be more affordable to live.

When it came to answering questions about him, Seth didn't like having to fabricate a story that wasn't true; however, he felt that he had no other choice. How could he possibly tell the truth about himself, and not expect her to jump out of the chair and make a quick escape from the lunatic sitting across from her? Seth said that he recently graduated Temple University in Philadelphia, and was now living with his dad, the writer, Adam Tiller. Her eyes lit up when she heard his name. She mentioned that all her guy friends read his books. She also said that her Uncle Joe has been a big fan of his for years, and hoped that one day she could meet him.

Seth had mixed feelings about her knowledge of his dad, and of her enthusiasm. He was delighted at the end of their conversation, when she considered meeting up with him again, but was mortified by the idea of wanting to meet his dad. Little did she know that she had already met the esteemed author of detective novels. She could have easily been given an autograph for her Uncle Joe! Seth explained that he took after his father in becoming a writer, but was not interested in the same literary genre. Thinking that it would improve his status, Seth told her that he had just started to read *The Lucky One*. Once again, her eyes lit up. She confessed that she was a huge fan of Nicholas Sparks, and had read all his books. He smiled as she gave him a bit of advice, "You'll be a great author, if you can learn to write like him."

Seth knew within his heart that there was something special about this woman, and that it ever there was a case for "love at first sight;" this was a classic one. He felt awful that the relationship had to start with such deceit, but he believed that she'd understand, once he eventually told her the truth. It would take some time before he'd be able to tell her who he really was, and only after she could learn the type of person he was.

Neither of the couple had much to eat for they were more concerned with learning about each other, than what was on the table in front of them. Seth couldn't imagine how a woman as beautiful as she, didn't have a boyfriend, or did she? She didn't wear an engagement or wedding ring, but it didn't mean that she wasn't dating someone. Seth didn't have to ponder this thought very long for she put an end to his curiosity.

The woman opened up to Seth sensing that she could trust him. She told him that she met a guy at NYC in her freshman year, and had seriously dated him over the last two years. She was devastated when she discovered that he was seeing another woman. When she confronted him about it, he told her that it wasn't what she thought it was, and that she meant everything to him. She elected to give him another chance, but called it quits when she saw him two weeks later with the same girl at a local night club; acting more toward each other than just being cordial. Her warm brown eyes began to fill, and a stream of tears started to flow down her cheeks. Seth handed her a clean napkin, and took her tenderly by the hand saying, "You weren't meant for each other. When you meet the right man; it will all make sense."

What he heard her say next, almost jolted him out of the chair. She shared that she had been praying to God ever since the two split up, to send her a man who would not only be her lover, but also her soul mate and best friend. Seth excused himself saying that he had to use the restroom, but really had to process her remark. He looked in the mirror at the sink, and pondered the possibilities. *Could I be the answer to her prayer? Is she the reason why I was compelled to return to Manhattan? Are we meant for each other?* He felt implored to tell her the truth about himself, but he concluded that it wasn't the time or the place. Besides, he needed to be sure. He had only known her for an hour, and didn't think that it was long enough to take a different kind of plunge.

When he returned to the table, Seth called the waiter for the check. He asked if she'd have dinner with him on Friday night. She, once again, accepted his invitation with no hesitancy. When he suggested that they exchange phone numbers, Seth became extremely embarrassed that he had never asked the woman her name. A bit of Adam Tiller must still have remained. She laughed, and told him that it wasn't a big deal. If what she had already revealed to him wasn't enough to knock him off the chair, what she would say next certainly would. "My name is Eva . . . Eva LoPresti."

Her first name was close enough to *Eve*, created by God using the rib of the first man. "Bone from my bones and flesh from my flesh," as described by the inspired writer of the Book of Genesis, and meant to emphasize the point that they were made for each other. *Was Eva made for me? Is she to return with me to Mirror Lake to start a new, innocent, and redeemed generation of mankind?*

Seth tried not to show any evidence of the shock that was now traveling throughout his entire body. He must not have done a very good job hiding it for she asked if there was anything wrong. He was quick to answer, "No, there is nothing wrong. I just thought for a moment that I had heard your name before." Had he decided to be honest with her, and tell Eva his real name; he didn't doubt that she, too, would have felt the same way.

Chapter Nineteen

Meeting with Vincent Peale

$\int$ eth returned home from a most enjoyable lunch with Eva, and after writing both a grocery and clothing list, started out to spend the rest of the day at a chic men's clothing store and the supermarket. He couldn't stop thinking about Eva, and whether or not she was part of his destiny. He knew that eventually she had to learn the truth about him and Mirror Lake. He was exuberant about his date with her on Friday, and thought of buying flowers and choosing the perfect place for dinner. He also pondered if this should be the best time to reveal to her the secret of Mirror Lake. By the time he returned to his apartment with a carload of new clothes and groceries, he had decided that it would be best to date her for a few weeks before opening up. In this way a sense of trust could develop in the relationship, and he'd know for certain whether or not Eva LoPresti was truly *the one*.

He spent the evening putting away clothes, filling the food pantry, and sifting through a basket of snail mail, as well as a ton of e-mails. He had a sudden urge to chat with Eva before he started to prepare dinner, so decided to call her number. He was disappointed when she didn't answer, but left a voice message. He said that he enjoyed lunch with her, and was looking forward to seeing her again on Friday night. After he ate, Seth sat on the sofa, and entered the day's entry in his journal. He couldn't say enough about Eva. It was close to ten o'clock, when he finally heard from her, but it was well worth the wait. She apologized for not returning his call sooner, but she and her roommate had gone to see *Wicked* on Broadway, and that she couldn't use her phone during the performance. Seth's heart fluttered as he listened to Eva describe the details of the popular and record-breaking musical performance. She was glad that he had called, and said that she was thinking of him all afternoon and evening. She mentioned him to her roommate, Lori, who having heard so much about him, couldn't wait to meet him.

The couple spoke for over an hour. They could have talked all night, if they didn't have to get up early in the morning. Seth discovered during their conversation, that her favorite food was Italian, and among a number of flowers she liked; sunflowers were her favorite. This knowledge made preparation for Friday's dinner a lot easier. Regarding her favorite food, it didn't surprise him that Italian was her favorite because it is the pick of many people he knew over the years. He wasn't disappointed for it was his favorite, too. He remembered telling a number of his Italian friends, *you don't have to be Italian to eat like one*! It was a cinch to choose the restaurant for their date. It would be Umberto's in the Little Italy section of the city. He had been there many times, and it was among his favorite Italian and seafood eateries in town. He planned to call the restaurant tomorrow to make reservations for eight o'clock on Friday.

Between his phone call and meeting up with her on Friday night, there was one unpleasant thing Seth had to do, and one to which he wasn't looking forward, namely, his meeting with Vincent Peale. The thought of this audience ruined what was up until now, a perfect day. The old publisher was a very perceptive individual, and could read a person like a book. If there was anyone who could figure out Seth's secret; it was Peale. He had to make sure that he wasn't going to slip up, as he did with the little boy at the airport. He had to be careful of words and expressions used by Adam, as well as specific mannerisms that could arouse the publisher's suspicion. It would be best to listen most of the time, and to say only what was minimally required.

Before he retired, Seth chose what he'd be wearing tomorrow for his meeting with Peale. Knowing that first impressions are lasting ones and determine the judgment made by people, he chose to wear one of the three new suits he purchased at the pricey men's clothing store on Fifth Avenue. After putting it aside, he showered, and read a few chapters of *The Lucky One* feeling very lucky in his own right. Although he wasn't due in Peale's office until ten a.m., he still had to rise early in the morning to continue his daily exercise schedule. He had found his MP3 earlier in the evening to which he'd listen as he jogged in Central Park. At one thirty a.m., it was time to call it a day. It was a most wonderful day! He took out his iPhone, and looked at a pic that he took of Eva in the café. He smiled and wished that he could meet her in his dreams.

The alarm clock blasted on the night table at six o'clock making Seth nearly jump out of bed. Even though he was able to get a mere four and a half hours of sleep, he felt more invigorated than yesterday. He knew that it had to do with Eva. He smiled to himself as he recalled an old David Cassidy hit of the sixties entitled *I Woke up in Love this Morning*. He, too, woke up in love, for he went to sleep with Eva on his mind. He jogged for an hour and a half in Central Park, showered, and whipped up a light breakfast. There would be no coffee. He was through with caffeine, once and for all. He hadn't taken care of his health as Adam Tiller, but was determined to do things right the second time around. He brushed his teeth, and then put on his suit. He never liked dressing up, and being in the wilderness for forty days made it worse. *God, it feels as if I'm wearing an iron lung!*

Seth took MTA from his apartment to the business district, where the Tiller Publishing House was located. Before he entered the building, he stopped at the "911" memorial, where the twin towers of the World Trade Center once stood. It was the most revered landmark in the city to all New Yorkers. He knew many people who perished in the most heinous act of terrorism on American soil, including his best friend, cousin, and the brother of his wife. He looked into the three-story waterfall pondering man's cruelty, and where the world seemed to be going. He thought of Mirror Lake, the second chance it had given to him, and possibly one day to all mankind. If there was ever a place that exemplified the need for man to be redeemed, it was on the hallowed ground where he was standing. Suddenly, everything made sense to him, and tears filled his eyes. It was during this moment, and at this special monument in history that Seth knew he must return to Mirror Lake with Eva to give humanity a second chance. Now, all he had to do was to convince her to join him.

Seth entered the publishing house with a bit of apprehension. As he walked to the elevator and along the fourth floor to Peale's office, not a single person he passed said anything to him, nor was he given as much as a suspicious glance. This was fine by him. As he stood in front of Peale's office, he took a deep breath, and reluctantly knocked on the door. He heard Peale yell, "Come in," so entered hoping that his meeting would be short, sweet, and most of all, one that wouldn't arouse Peale's suspicion. The publisher was sitting with his feet on the desk reading the *Wall Street Journal*. He looked over the newspaper, and signaled for Seth to come in. As he approached the desk, Peale stood up, and extended his hand to welcome him. After Seth introduced himself Peale, told him that it wasn't necessary for he was a "spitting image" of his father, and he'd be able to pick him out in a roomful of people. He asked how his dad was doing, and hoped that Seth would be able to tell him something about his new book.

Seth had to control himself from laughing as he said that his dad never looked healthier and younger, but as far as his book; he had kept that a secret even from his son. Seth didn't know what to say when he was asked how long he planned to live in his dad's apartment, so he ended up saying that it would be at least until his father returned in September. Peale was surprisingly kind to Seth, and suggested a number of affordable places in the city. Seth thought for sure that Peale would ask someone else to give him a tour of the building, so was surprised when he was told that the publishing giant would be doing the honor himself. Seth played along as if it was truly the first time he had been through the building, and did more listening than talking.

Peale mentioned that his father wanted to give him a job at the publishing house, but was honest when he added that he wasn't sure where Seth could best fit in. Seth didn't care if he was given the position as the night shift janitor, so long as he could get out of Peale's sight and get started with the tour. He resented Peale for the affair with his wife, and that he inherited the top job at the publishing house after Marie's death; however, he had decided to let it go in the hope of allowing her soul to rest in peace. He wasn't one who normally holds grudges, especially now more than ever. Besides, he was a firm believer in the ancient proverb, "What goes around comes around," so in time Peale would be eating his just dessert. Nevertheless, there was still a part of him that wanted to feed Peale himself!

Everything was going considerably well, until Seth was introduced to Marge Ritter, the top editor at the publishing house. She had set up just about every best seller that Adam Tiller had ever written. She was a sixty-four year old widow, who worked closely with the writer, and became his only true friend in the company. She knew Adam even better than he knew himself, so it made Seth nervous being around her. As Seth shook hands with Marge, a strange expression came over the woman's face. Could she have already known that he was really Adam Tiller? Or perhaps was she taken back by the remarkable resemblance that Seth shared with his father? Peale explained the reason for Seth coming to the publishing house, as Marge listened intently. She looked back and forth from the publisher to Seth in a very curious, if not dubious fashion. Seth was relieved as she finally excused herself, saying that she had to make an important phone call before heading to the cafeteria for lunch.

Seth almost had a stroke when Peale joined him in the elevator to the cafeteria, thinking that he planned to eat lunch with him. He was relieved when Peale told him that he was on his own for lunch, as they exited the elevator, but told him to stop by his office after he finished eating. Seth graciously thanked Peale for the tour, and shook his hand. *So far, so good.* He sat near a window that overlooked the "911" memorial and ordered a turkey club sandwich with a glass of lemonade. He looked around and recognized all the employees sitting throughout the cafeteria, many of whom he was influential in hiring. He looked down at his plate after having seen Marge Ritter enter the cafeteria.

He was mortified when he saw her walking directly to his table. She politely asked if she could join him. He wanted to say, *Can't you find another table, lady!* but reluctantly accepted her self-invitation. He expected her to start yelling and accuse him of being a fraud, but his nerves calmed as she began to speak lovingly of his father. He perceived that she was going to be his one and only ally at the publishing house; just as she had been to Adam. What she told Seth in their pleasant exchange was a startling revelation. She confessed that for years, she had a tremendous crush on his father, and that she felt sorry for him having, "to be stuck with that two-timing wife of his!" He wasn't the only one in the company who suspected that Marie was cheating on him. Seth was given every indication that she was planning to make a move, once Adam had grieved long enough over the death of his wife. In a way he felt sorry for Marge, knowing that she was never going to see Adam Tiller again. He offered to pay for lunch, but she politely refused his kind gesture. They left the cafeteria together, and took the elevator until she exited on a different floor from where he was heading.

Seth peered into the publisher's office, and saw that Peale was talking on the phone. When he saw Seth, he motioned for him to enter and take the chair in front of his desk. Apparently, it was a conversation that Peale didn't mind Seth hearing. After he hung up, Peale placed an employment form in front of Seth telling him that it was only a formality. All he had to do was to read it and sign it. Seth was handed a pen, and he signed the form as he had done for over fifty years—"Adam J. Tiller." Seth had made his first mistake, and it would prove to be a costly one. When Peale looked at the signature, he raised his eyebrows, and looked at Seth in disbelief. Now, aware of his blunder, Seth blushed, and began to squirm his way out of the hole he had dug for himself by making up some silly explanation that he knew Peale wasn't buying.

He signed another form, but this time as, "Seth A. Tiller," but the damage had already been done. He sat for a moment uncomfortably like a fish out of water, and didn't want to imagine what Peale was thinking. After a silence that seemed to last for an eternity, Peale said, "I suppose your middle initial stands for Adam?" Seth nodded. He then told Seth that he was to report to work tomorrow at eight o'clock sharp. What Peale had chosen for the son of his best selling author, would be far worse than the night shift janitorial position.

Chapter Twenty

Obstacles along the Way

Seth was disappointed when told that he'd be working in the copy-editing department. He knew that it was a punishment, now that there was suspicion brewing in Peale's mind. He didn't want to make things worse by asking for a different position, and certainly didn't want Peale to ask him any more questions. All he wanted to do was to get out. He hated having to edit someone's work. He was a writer, and accustomed to giving his manuscript to someone else to edit. At least he'd be working for Marge Ritter. Seth knew that Peale wasn't through with him, and things were going to get a lot hairier. This meant that he had to approach Eva about the truth sooner than later. Seth thanked Peale, and stood up hoping to bring this disturbing audience to an end. As he made his way to the door, Peale stopped him abruptly in his tracks, and told him that there was more thing he had to do. Seth held his breath and without turning around listened to Peale as he demanded the submission of a complete résumé of his college and work experiences, including personal and business references. Seth turned around as Peale concluded with a mischievous grin, "Don't worry, Adam, er . . . I mean, Seth. It is only a formality."

Seth left the office with a knot in his stomach, and sweat pouring down his back. When he returned home, he poured a tall glass of iced tea, picked up his laptop, and flopped on his lounge chair. He had to contrive a résumé, and had no idea where to start. *How in the world am I going to pull off such a stunt? Everything has to be faked. What will happen if Peale chooses to call one of my references?* He thought of calling Lucci to ask him to be a reference, but other than Lucci; there was no other person who'd go along with his caper. The only recourse he had was to stall. He decided to fabricate an excuse that his dad's printer wasn't working. That would give him at least a few days. He hoped that Peale wouldn't request that he submit it electronically. He wouldn't know how to weasel his way out of that one. He sat as in a catatonic position. He never expected to find himself in such a pickle. *Is this God's way of telling me to leave Manhattan now, and head back to Mirror Lake? Maybe God is making the decision for me, since I seem to be screwing things up on my own!*

The only relief that Seth would experience this night was when he spoke to Eva on the phone. Hearing her sweet voice was the best medicine to remedy the ill-feeling resulting from his meeting with Peale. If only he hadn't made that awful signature blunder! Seth had very little to say when Eva asked about how things went at the publishing house, and quickly changed the subject. He had an itch to start talking about Mirror Lake, but chose to hold off until Friday. After speaking with Eva for almost an hour, he showered, and watched the evening news. He thought of fishing on Mirror Lake, and enjoying a beautiful sunset with Eva at his side. After eating a light meal, he sprawled on the sofa thinking about what tomorrow would bring, and then typed his journal entry. He made his way to the bedroom, sat up in bed with *The Lucky One* in his hands, and feeling anything but lucky. He read the book to its entirety hoping to prevent a night of insomnia. He dreaded going to work tomorrow.

The first thing that Seth did the next morning at the publishing house was to report to Peale's office. He told him as planned that he couldn't produce the résumé because his dad's printer wasn't working. Peale didn't seem too concerned, but asked him to sit down for a minute. Seth wasn't comfortable sitting in the hot seat, and tried to keep Peale from sensing that he was really stewing. The publisher began to ask him questions about the courses he had taken at Temple in the guise that it would help him to arrive at the best position in the publishing house. Seth figured that he was only grilling him in an effort to trip him up, and catch him in a lie. He asked about his college professors, hinting that he might know a number of them. Seth nervously spun another one of his yarns, until he felt as if he dug himself into a deep hole in which he'd never be able to escape. He had to resort to the creation of fictitious names, when Peale asked him to name a few of his professors. Seth was convinced that Peale was going to call Temple the minute he left the office, and when he discovered that there wasn't a single teacher Seth mentioned on the faculty, he'd pound the final nail in his coffin. Mirror Lake never sounded better.

After Peale's own version of the Spanish Inquisition finally came to an end, he ordered Seth to report to Mrs. Ritter. Seth immediately sprung to his feet, and started for the door. He was fortunate to have survived this round with minimal damage, yet he knew that the next one could conceivably earn him a Purple Heart! Marge was happy that Adam's son would be working in her department, and couldn't be any nicer to him. The week flew by without Peale grilling Seth, or asking for his résumé. He wasn't certain if that was a good or bad thing.

The excitement was mounting, as he drove home from work on Friday. He couldn't wait to see Eva. He rehearsed what he was going to say about Mirror Lake all day, while he sat in his cubicle; however, he couldn't just come right out and tell her about it in the middle of eating a bowl of minestrone soup. He thought of feeding her a few glasses of wine before dropping the bomb. As much as he felt comfortable talking to Eva, he truly didn't know her well enough to start talking about living with him forever at some underwater paradise. It takes time to nurture a trusting relationship, but time was one thing that wasn't on his side; given the situation with Peale. He had fallen head over heels for Eva, but he wasn't sure how she felt about him. He wasn't convinced that she'd be ready and willing *to row into the sunset* with him.

Perhaps Seth was reading too much into what Peale might do, or worse had already done. Worrying about it didn't seem to be helping, so he decided to keep Peale off his mind at least for tonight. As Seth showered and dressed for his first date in decades, he had to admit that he was feeling a bit nervous. He didn't seem to mind the butterflies in his stomach for he read it as a sign that he was a different man, who enjoyed being in love again. He chose to dress formally, wearing a pair of dress slacks, a shirt, tie, and a sports jacket. He arrived promptly to Eva's place at seven o'clock.

Eva's roommate opened the door, and welcomed Seth into her apartment. She told him that Eva was still getting dressed, and invited him to sit down with her in the living room. He found the young woman to be pleasant, and by her reaction, he must have been everything that Eva told her that he'd be. About ten minutes later Eva entered the room. She looked absolutely stunning. If the room was dim, she'd certainly have lit it up with her radiant presence. She wore a tight red dress that looked as if she had been poured into it. She wore her hair up, and on the side of it was a beautiful red flower. She wore a pearl necklace with matching earrings. If Seth was made of butter, he would have surely melted. After a brief conversation, Lori gave both of them a big hug and a kiss, and told them to have a wonderful time.

Seth and Eva sat at the bar in Umberto's until their table was available. Eva had an iced tea, and Seth, a diet Coke with a twist of lemon. They had a delightful dinner. For the most part, Eva did most of the talking. That suited Seth fine in light of the fact that he had no personal history to share. He stumbled over a few questions that Eva asked about his childhood, and was uneasy when she wanted to know about his mother and father. He felt awful having to either stretch the truth, or at times totally fabricate a lie. Again, he was confident that she would understand, once he introduced her to the secret of Mirror Lake. Talking about it was more difficult than he had anticipated, and even though Peale was hastening his time table, Seth deemed that tonight wasn't the right time to bring it up. *It will only spoil the delightful time that we are having.*

There was no doubt in his mind that Eva liked him. He saw it in her eyes, facial expressions, and heard it in her voice. He sensed that she, too, was falling in love with him. Before Seth took her home, they enjoyed a stroll in Central Park; often walking hand in hand. Seth suggested that they do something together tomorrow, so after a brief discussion they settled for a place to visit that they both agreed was a favorite—The Metropolitan Museum of Art. As they neared the end of their walk, Eva told Seth how much she enjoyed dinner. They stood gazing into each other's eyes, until Seth made a move to kiss her. He didn't see fireworks, but knew for certain that she was *the one.* He could only hope that Eva had a similar feeling. After driving her home, they exchanged another and more passionate caress at the door of the apartment. Seth would have preferred joining "Mrs. Tiller" inside their house, but sadly had to head back to his own apartment alone.

As Seth lie in bed, he relived the entire evening with Eva. On one hand, he easily imagined that she would have no problem choosing a life with him, even if she'd have to leave New York and a possible job with Merrill Lynch. Yet, on the other hand, he thought that she could easily label him as a "nut case," and refuse to see him anymore. He speculated how he'd feel if Eva would be the one to bring up such a fanciful story, and whether or not *he'd* believe *her*. He came to the conclusion that telling her about Mirror Lake wasn't the way to go, but rather, *taking* her there was a far better option. Once Eva saw the underwater cavern; she would have no other choice than to believe his story. However, even if she would believe it, there was no guarantee that she would choose to live there with Seth. It was too much for anyone to ask, unless of course, Eva truly loved him.

Before falling asleep, Seth vowed that he would no longer lie or stretch the truth. If Eva would ask about his past, he'd simply deflect the conversation to his future; particularly, one that he'd hope to share with her. He considered asking Eva how she felt about him, rather than to assume any feelings for her. He thought that they should hold off any serious conversation at the MET, and wait until Sunday after Mass when he could invite her to his apartment and spill the beans. Tomorrow would be a day for Seth to enjoy the treasures of the museum, as well as the treasure he had discovered in the person of Eva LoPresti.

Their trip to the museum was most enjoyable. Eva had as much a taste for Egyptian mummies as did Seth. She was impressed with what Seth knew about ancient Egypt. He almost fell off a bench when she commented, "You have the knowledge of a man more advanced in age." Seth was equally impressed with Eva's knowledge of Art. It wasn't surprising; having already been told that she minored in Art at NYC. Seth boasted about the Philadelphia Museum of Art, and when Eva told him all she knew about it was that Sylvester Stallone ran up its steps in the movie *Rocky*, he suggested that they visit it one day. It seemed for the time being that Seth had forgotten about Mirror Lake, his job, and Vincent Peale. That is the way Eva made him feel.

Nothing was more important than being with her. She was the center of his attention, and the meaning in his life. If only she felt the same way about him.

Seth didn't want the day to come to an end, so invited Eva to his apartment a day sooner than he had anticipated. She was extremely impressed by what she saw, but was disappointed when she found out that Seth's dad wasn't there. When she asked where he was, Seth kept his self-promise that he wouldn't tell a lie, and said that he was involved with writing a new book. It was enough to allay her curiosity. As the couple sat on the sofa sipping Perrier, they continued an earlier conversation concerning how the Egyptians built the great pyramids having only a primitive level of technology. She was extremely intrigued, as Seth spoke about large wooden sledges that could have been used to pull the large limestone blocks. He also joked about a theory that aliens provided the Egyptians with the know-how.

During their conversation, Seth noticed that Eva looked over to the bar a couple of times, and suspected that she wanted a drink. He recalled that she had no alcoholic beverage at dinner. He didn't think it would be polite not offering one to her, even though he had no intention of joining her. After he finished his discourse on Egyptian engineering, he offered her a drink. She declined his offer and settled for another Perrier. After taking a sip, she began to share a sadness that she experienced in her childhood. She confessed that her father was an alcoholic, and had physically and emotionally abused her mother. She vowed at a very young age never to start drinking; having learned from her own experience of its adverse effects. Seth wasn't surprised when Eva told him that her parents divorced when she was eleven years old. She hadn't seen her dad since he left, but heard that he was remarried and now living in Connecticut.

Eva also revealed that her mother has ovarian cancer, and was given only a few months to live. Mrs. LoPresti moved in about a year ago with her sister, who lives in Narberth, Pennsylvania. That is where Eva planned to temporarily reside after her internship, if she wasn't offered a job with Merrill Lynch. She told Seth that she visits her mother every weekend, and was going tomorrow. This shot a hole in Seth's plan. He felt like a child, who just had the air deflated from his balloon. He had to, once again, postpone talking about Mirror Lake. *How can I imagine that Eva would ever think of leaving her dying mother, even for Mirror Lake?* Eva sensed that there was a change in Seth's mood, so asked what was wrong. Seth said that he really felt bad for Eva's mother; that was all. Once again, he had reverted back to being untruthful. For the first time since he had met Eva, Seth had a feeling of despair. If he did choose to return to Mirror Lake, it seemed that he'd be going there by himself.

Seth was originally going to ask Eva to stay for dinner. Now, he needed time to be alone, so he could think things over. Eva didn't live very far away, so Seth chose to walk her home. He could utilize the stroll back to clear his head, and to come up with some alternate plan. Eva invited him in, perhaps wanting to cook dinner for him, but he declined her offer. Instead of kissing as passionately as before, he gave her a peck on the lips. She had to be wondering, *What on earth has happened?* Seth told Eva to have a safe trip to Narberth, and that he'd say a prayer for her mother at Saint Patrick's in the morning. He took his time walking back to the apartment mulling things over. He knew deep inside, that he could easily spend the rest of his life with Eva, but didn't think that it would be at Mirror Lake. He expected to be using the rest of the night and all day tomorrow, reconstructing his future. One thing was certain; he wanted Eva to be part of it, but wasn't sure where it would exactly be.

Chapter Twenty-One

Love is in the Air

Seth sat on a bench at Central Park in deep thought. He toyed with the idea of calling Eva to ask if he could join her tomorrow. Perhaps it would provide a lift for her mother, seeing that her daughter had rebounded from the painful break-up with her ex-boyfriend, and was now dating another man. By the time he arrived at his apartment the decision was made; he was going to do it. Eva was ecstatic to hear that Seth was interested in spending the day with her in Narberth, and unknown to Seth, had shed tears while speaking with him on the phone. He offered to be the one to drive, and asked what time she'd want him to get her. Eva told him that she wanted to attend the eight a.m. Mass at Saint Patrick's before she left, so it looked like Seth would be attending Mass with her after all.

When he finished talking with Eva, he wondered why she'd still be attending Mass. *Wasn't I, the answer to her prayer?* The thought troubled Seth for he hoped that Eva had the same sentiments for him, as he had for her. *She could be going to Mass to pray for her mother or to thank God for sending me to her?* This latter thought brought a smile to his face.

Seth was at her apartment at seven-thirty, and they drove to the cathedral in his car. Eva lit two candles after Mass. She would tell Seth later, that one was for her mother, and the other was for a prayer that had been answered. Seth concluded that *he* had to be that answered prayer! On their way to Narberth, Eva spoke about her mother, and how she resented her father for deserting them. Apparently, Eva had no siblings for none were mentioned in her conversation. Seth was content with the fact that she was doing most of the talking. The less he'd have to convey about his family, the better.

Seth asked Eva to find a radio station they both liked, so after scanning the stations for a minute, she came to the perfect New York country music station. As they arrived in Pennsylvania, she found the one to which she listens every weekend when she travels to visit her mother. Even though Seth was in essence, forty years older than Eva, country music was a common thread to which they could connect. Albeit he enjoyed traditional country music, he also liked the new breed of country artists, too. It seemed that the more he learned about Eva, the more he discovered they had in common. He did, however, come upon a sore spot and Seth knew he'd have his work cut out in dealing with it. She, too, liked baseball, but she didn't root for the same team as Seth. She was an avid fan of the New York Mets!

It didn't take much for Seth to fall in love with Eva's mother. She was the Italian mother that every non-Italian boy dreams of having. She was beautiful, a great cook, kept a squeaky clean house, and had a heart as big as the Empire State Building. He was glad that he had chosen to accompany Eva. As the day progressed, it was obvious that Mrs. LoPresti liked him. After a delicious lunch that included home-made cheese ravioli and meatballs, the trio took a stroll in a local park. Seth liked the town's quaintness, character, and quiet. It was the kind of place where he'd consider settling down and raising a family. When they returned to the house, Seth met Eva's aunt, who was as delightful and bubbly as her sister. They sat over a cup of coffee, and a variety of home-made Italian cookies that were the best that Seth had ever tasted. He passed on the coffee, and had a glass of iced tea instead. Not for a single instance, did Mrs. LoPresti complain about any aches or pains, even though Seth knew that she had to be feeling a great deal of discomfort. If there was anyone who could beat cancer; it was her. She had a very positive attitude about her illness, and seemed to possess a strong faith that could simply *will* the disease away.

As Eva was in her room gathering a few things to take back home with her and her aunt busy cleaning up in the kitchen, Mrs. LoPresti sat with Seth in the living room. She told him how happy she was that her daughter had met him, and that she sensed a good chemistry between them. She then, told Seth something that surprised him. "I have a strong feeling that the two of you are meant for each other," she said in an assuring tone. It was certainly sweet music to Seth's ears, and confirmed his own feeling about Eva and him. His response was contrite, and seemed to have pleased her mother. "I believe that you are right, Mrs. LoPresti, for I feel the same way. And with that being said,

I promise to take good care of her for the rest of her life." A vibrant smile radiated from the sick woman's face that was just as olive-colored and wrinkle-free as her daughter's. It was a smile that Seth would never forget, nor would he sadly ever see again.

When Eva returned to the living room, her mother excused herself and went to the kitchen to prepare a "goody bag" for both Eva and Seth that included pasta and meatballs, as well as Italian cookies. As the couple sat alone on the sofa, Eva asked how he liked her mother. His kind response brought a smile to Eva's face; one that Seth realized she inherited from her dear mother. A sudden sadness came over him, as he thought about her illness and prognosis. *She would make a wonderful mother-in-law and an awesome grandmother.* There was also sadness in Eva's eyes although she was still smiling. Seth couldn't imagine the tremendous amount of pain that was harboring within her heart. *How could she ever think of leaving her loving mother, even if she'd be with me?*

Mrs. LoPresti hugged and kissed them both, and told Seth to come again. Eva's Aunt Mildred, also gave them a round of hugs and kisses, and likewise invited Seth back. On the way home Eva couldn't thank Seth enough for coming with her. He responded by telling her that the pleasure was his. Although not very hungry after having a satisfying lunch, Seth still suggested that they stop for something to eat before returning home. Eva wasn't very hungry either, yet like Seth, didn't want their wonderful day to come to an end. They chose to stop at a chic café on Fifth Avenue, and as was the case before; they ended up doing more chatting than eating.

At the table, Eva thanked him, once again, for accompanying her. She sensed that her mother really liked Seth, and told him that his presence had lifted her spirit. He was glad to hear this for it was his primary intention, but he also did it for Eva. He could see that her spirit was also lifted. Seth tried to reason how any man could ever hurt his wife and daughter, especially as beautiful and loving as Mrs. LoPresti and Eva? Mankind had truly missed the mark, and was in desperate need of redemption. When Eva excused herself to go to the restroom, Seth began to dig deep within himself. *As a Catholic, I believe that God sent His only Son to save humanity from their sins, but it was solely, a spiritual redemption. Isn't this obvious by the fact that mankind doesn't appear any different on the outside after Jesus died and rose from the dead? Baptism washes away sins on souls. Ashes on the forehead at the beginning of Lent are only a reminder of a person's need to repent. For Christ's coming to be totally fruitful, mankind needs to change both on the inside and outside. The acid test for authentic change can only be seen by how a person treats another human being. I wouldn't want to be in the shoes of Eva's dad on Judgment Day!*

In short, Seth believed that man needed to be redeemed on a temporal order as well as on a spiritual one. He surmised that Reverend Moon may have been on the right track in marrying those couples at a single setting; engrafting them into God's sinless lineage. Seth felt that he and Eva could be destined to start this new order, as the first parents of a redeemed mankind. The love they'd share would be pure and unconditional. They would teach their children to love, and to treat all people with dignity and respect. Mirror Lake never seemed more logical and necessary to Seth. Why else would God have created a perfect place within the world that He already set in motion? The answer was as clear as a bell to him. He might well be excommunicated by the Pope for this belief, but it seemed so right. How did he know if this wasn't part of the mysterious "third secret of Fatima" that he once read about? The Pope might decide not to excommunicate him after all, but dub him a Papal Knight!

Upon Eva's return to the table, she began to share the sentiments that she had for Seth. He was touched by her words, and knew they were issuing from a sincere and loving heart. She brought back into their dialogue, the second candle that she had lit earlier at Saint Patrick's. She reechoed that it was in thanksgiving for an answered prayer, but this time she admitted that Seth was the answer to that prayer! She told him that she could see a future life together, and that her mother agreed. Seth laughed when he heard that, and told Eva that she said the same thing to him when alone in the living room.

Since Eva had opened up to Seth, it was also time for Seth to do likewise. He shared the ardor he had her, and articulated how much she meant to him. He almost went as far as revealing the secret of Mirror Lake, but something inside of him said that it wasn't the appropriate time to do so. He still had more thinking to do, but after meeting Mrs. LoPresti and hearing what Eva had to say; a life together at Mirror Lake was beginning to look more promising. He had to be patient, and had to time things perfectly. Most importantly, he had to trust that God was in control and that in *His* time; all things would come together for his good, Eva's, and for all mankind.

Eva insisted that she pay the check for dinner. She argued that Seth used his car, paid for the tolls and gas, and that he always seemed to pay for the meals. "It is no more than fair that I pay this time," she said in earnest. He reminded her that he was the son of a millionaire, and that she was only an intern hoping to be hired by Merrill Lynch; however, she held her ground. Seth finally gave in, and let Eva pay the bill. They walked back to the car holding hands, and then Seth drove her home. The couple walked to the front door, still not wanting the day to end. Eva thanked him one last time for spending the day with her. As she told Seth that she loved him, he lowered the bag he was carrying to the ground, wrapped his arms around her back, and gave her a tender kiss on the lips. Whatever was missing in the last kiss was surely present in this one! Seth told Eva that he loved her as well, and believed that she was going to be a definite part of his future. Revealing the secret of Mirror Lake didn't appear to be very far off.

At home, Seth transferred the leftovers from the grocery bag to his refrigerator, took out his laptop, and at the kitchen table completed his journal entry for the day. All the pieces seemed to be coming together, and even though he wasn't totally convinced that Eva would chose to spend the rest of her life with him at Mirror Lake, he was sure that she was going to spend it with him somewhere.

He walked into the living room, and sat on his recliner. Closing his eyes, he recounted the day in Narberth, and the conversations with Eva in the car and the restaurant. His pleasant thoughts were interrupted by an incoming text from Eva. She told him that she had a wonderful time, missed him already, and that she loved him. He returned her text with one word—"Ditto." He liked being Seth Tiller, and for the first time since he had concocted the name and person; felt comfortable being him. *Is this the end of Adam Tiller for sure?* Seth was ready and willing to spend the rest of eternity with Eva, and had no qualms about laying his former self to rest. He even had an obituary written up for the occasion.

Seth closed his eyes again. He began to consider when it would be the best time and place to tell Eva about Mirror Lake. *How could I get her to return with me and see it for herself?* He didn't want to coerce her into coming and eventually to stay with him, but rather, he wanted her to freely choose for herself. Seth presumed that she would be knocked out of her socks when she'd see the underwater cavern, and wouldn't need any arm-twisting. Timing was everything; yet time wasn't on the side of Eva's mother. Seth had to swallow hard when he imagined that despite all Mirror Lake and he had to offer, Eva could never leave her mother as long as she was alive. Could he really blame her? He didn't mind waiting for Eva, as long as Peale wasn't on his back, and if Lucci would continue to be patient with him.

Seth thought that if Eva would see Mirror Lake for only a few hours that she'd be captivated by its magic, and would want to join him sooner or later. The possibility of Eva agreeing to go for a short visit prompted Seth to book a flight for Friday night with a return flight scheduled for early Sunday morning, so Eva could still make her weekly trip to see her mother. He was convinced that all Eva needed was one full day at Mirror Lake to understand what he had been unsuccessfully trying to tell her.

Seth envisioned how their stay at Mirror Lake would go. He imagined walking in the woods, fishing on the lake and taking in a beautiful sunset, enjoying a romantic dinner, and finally taking *the plunge* with her to the underwater cavern. He didn't think that Mrs. LoPresti would mind that her daughter would spend a couple of days with him. She told Seth herself that he and Eva were meant for each other; however, Seth had to respect Eva's wishes. If she chose not to join him for the weekend, he would honor her decision, and should she choose not to join him at Mirror Lake at all, Seth would have no other option than to tell her about it. He didn't think that it was the best path to take knowing that a picture, and in this case *being there*, would be worth more than a thousand words!

An important key to Seth's plan, if Eva chose not to join him at Mirror Lake until her mother passed on, was Vincent Peale. As long as he exerted no pressure on him, Seth was ready to wait it out. If there was a threat to his identity; he'd be forced to leave for the lake without Eva, hoping that she'd eventually meet up with him. It wasn't going to be very long before he'd find out exactly what Peale had decided to do about this strange young man, who mysteriously walked into Tiller's Publishing House, and claiming to be the son of the publisher's most wealthy and popular client.

Chapter Twenty-Two

A Fly in the Ointment

For the next couple of days, it was business as usual at the publishing house. Seth put in his hours at the office during the day, and spoke to Eva each night. It wasn't the most exciting work, but it kept Peale at a distance. He had a hard time trying to muster the courage to invite Eva to Mirror Lake, and time was running out. Since he booked a flight for Friday night, he had to bring it up no later than Thursday, and that might be too short a notice. Peale stopped by Seth's cubicle on Wednesday afternoon with something that Seth had feared, yet wasn't expecting. It would change Seth's plan and time table drastically.

Seth was blown out of the water. Peale must have called Temple to do a background check. He accused him of being an imposter and worse, accused him of foul play. Peale was departing for an out of state publisher's convention, and gave Seth until Monday to explain himself, or the police would be notified. Seth tried to keep his composure, and did his best to keep from panicking.

He lodged no defense, and chose to remain silent; not wanting to let the situation escalate into something worse. All Seth needed was to weather the present storm, and once he was safely out of the publishing house; initiate an emergency response to Peale's ultimatum.

Mrs. Ritter overheard Peale's accusation and threat. When the publisher left, she asked if there was anything that she could do. Seth thanked her for her concern, and said that he was fine. He had a strange feeling that somehow she knew everything, and unlike Peale had chosen to ignore it. She was the only person that Seth was going to miss.

Seth couldn't wait to leave and to call Eva. He remained at the publishing house until quitting time, and planned to call her when he knew that she'd be at home. Eva had just walked through the door of the apartment when Seth hit the speed button feature on his phone. She heard a sense of urgency in his voice, so of course agreed to meet him later in the evening. The best place to speak privately was at his apartment. She didn't mind driving over. He told her not to worry about dinner for he'd be ordering out. Eva said that she'd be over in ninety minutes, and when asked what kind of food she preferred, she told him that anything would be fine.

They had chatted in the past about favorite foods, and Seth learned that in addition to Italian, she also liked Chinese food. Seth decided to order while still holding the phone in his hand. He knew that Eva's favorite dishes were also favored by him, namely, moo goo gai pan, pork fried rice, and chicken with broccoli. In addition to these entrees, he also ordered two egg rolls, wonton soup, and a rack of baby spare ribs. In light of the meals they had actually eaten in the past, he knew that he had over-ordered; but it really didn't matter.

He set the dining room table with his finest china, so not to eat out of the white delivery cartons. He set up a pair of crystal candlesticks to create a romantic ambiance. He finally took out two sets of chopsticks in the event that Eva knew how to use them. He reminisced of the time he and Marie traveled to Hong Kong almost thirty years ago, and had learned how to use them in a genuine Chinese restaurant. Noticing that something was missing, Seth stormed out of his apartment building. He ran down the street to a florist shop where he purchased a fresh arrangement of sunflowers for the dinner table. Upon his return, he took a quick shower, and put on something more casual and relaxing to wear. Within seconds of his arrival to the kitchen the door bell rang; it was his delivery of Chinese food. Before he could do much with the food Eva arrived. He gave her the biggest hug and kiss that added to her suspicion that something was wrong. They sat in the living room for a few minutes, and chatted about small things until he decided that it was time to eat. He excused himself for a brief moment to prepare the food and to light the candles. In the meantime, Eva paged thoughtlessly through a book of Art Deco that was sitting on the coffee table, while trying to conjecture why Seth had called her over.

When Seth was ready, he invited Eva to join him in the dining room. She grinned when she saw the lighted candles, and joked that Seth must have gone out of his way preparing such a fine Chinese dinner. Eva confessed that she never used chopsticks, so was given a free lesson. Seth congratulated her for doing a fine job using them, even though she managed to drop some food on her plate, and once on her lap. It was then, that she chose to finish her meal with more conventional American cutlery. Seth totally forgot about dessert, and didn't want the fortune cookie that came with dinner to be all he'd serve. After he cleared the table, Seth put a tray of Mrs. LoPresti's home-made Italian cookies on the table and offered coffee, tea, or a cold beverage. Eva joked by telling Seth that his cookies were as good, if not better, than her mom's! By the end of the meal, and with all joking aside, Eva thanked Seth for a delicious dinner. She helped him to clean up despite his protest. As they washed the dishes, both enjoyed a *soap suds* war that ended in a truce sealed by a kiss at the sink. It was obvious that Eva had fallen head over heels for Seth, but would it be enough for her to drop everything, and fly with him to Wisconsin on such short notice? What if she already had something important planned?

Seth felt odd in a way, not having an alcoholic beverage with meals, especially when dining with a woman. It was a help that Eva wasn't a drinker, but he wouldn't be able to get her mellow before dropping the bomb. As he prepared two glasses of iced tea in the kitchen while Eva waited in the living room, he recalled a conversation many years ago that he and his dad had about excessive drinking. Mister Tiller believed that there was no reason his son had to attain an *alcohol-induced* high, when he possessed a cheerful personality, and able to attain a *natural* high. If only he had listened to his dad about drinking, and so many other things about life. He was as guilty as the teens of today, who think that their parents are *old-fashioned* or just simply out of touch. If only he was able to appreciate the wisdom of his parents; learning not only by their advice, but more importantly, from their example. He was now; however, determined to use the second chance that he was given and not to take the same path in life that had led him to perdition. With two glasses of iced tea in his hands, he joined Eva in the living room ready to go.

Seth thought about how he was going to approach the topic of Mirror Lake for days, rehearsed exactly what he planned to say, yet it still was difficult to get started. He asked how Eva's day went, then prefaced his remarks by asking that she trust him for what he was about to ask. Eva's intuition was correct, and she braced herself for what came next. He started by telling her about the place where he had been for a month and a half, but did not say anything about the underwater cavern. Eva listened intently and saw how excited Seth was talking about it. She wasn't necessarily an outdoors person, and didn't have much experience camping or hiking in the woods to make a fair judgment. The more Seth talked about the northwoods and Mirror Lake, the more Eva seemed to like it, and so it didn't surprise Seth when she said that she'd like to visit it one day. She had no clue that Seth was soon going to suggest that the *one day* be the upcoming weekend!

Seth took a deep breath, and with hopeful anticipation, invited her to spend the weekend with him at Mirror Lake. At first, she was stunned by his invitation, but any reservation she had was soon replaced with the excitement of spending a weekend with the man she loved dearly. Thoughts of what she and Seth might do filled her mind. *It sounds as if it can be a lot of fun, and romantic at the same time!* Coming back to reality, she asked, "Are you sure that we will be back in time for me to visit my mother?" Seth promised that they would be back in time, but it would involve a substantial amount of traveling. He also offered to go with her for a second time, and would once again do the driving.

It was a lot for Eva to think about, and she had little time to give Seth an answer. She gave herself a few extra minutes to think about it, by excusing herself to use the restroom. She wanted to spend the weekend with Seth, but didn't want everything to be rushed in order to visit her mother. In light of her mother's present stable condition, she chose to forgo the visit. She knew that her mother would understand, especially since it involved going somewhere with Seth. When Eva told him of her decision, Seth didn't want her to skip the visit. Eva insisted that her mother wouldn't mind. To make it easier for Seth, she called her mother from the apartment and after listening to the conversation between mother and daughter; he felt better. When she finished speaking to her mother, Seth told her that once she saw Mirror Lake, she'd understand the sense of urgency to get there. He promised that she'd be amazed by its beauty, and that there was a special surprise in store for her.

Seth was ecstatic when Eva consented to his hasty plan. He could understand why she was in a hurry to get back to her apartment for she needed to make the necessary preparations. He told her that the flight was scheduled for eight o'clock, and that an airport van would be picking her up at six. She told him that she'd work through her usual one hour lunch break in order to leave work earlier.

She thanked Seth for the delicious meal. Seth grinned mischievously and replied, "Yeah, you have no idea how much I slaved over the stove preparing it!" He could see how excited Eva was about going, and that made him more excited as well.

Closing the door as Eva departed; he put his back to the door and giving a fist pump, cried out, "Yes!" He had worried so much about Eva's response, yet she consented with such little apprehension. He was grateful to Mrs. LoPresti, who must have known how much Eva wanted and *needed* to go with him. He sat on the sofa pleased by the way dinner turned out. As he typed in his daily journal entry, he could feel the excitement continue to mount. When he left Mirror Lake, he wasn't certain if he'd ever be returning. He didn't imagine in his wildest dreams that if he did return, it would be with Eva and in such a short period of time. He had no doubt in his mind that Mirror Lake would be as enchanting to her as it had been to him.

He went online to check the weather forecast for both New York and Wisconsin, and was glad to see that there was no threat of any thunderstorm activity. In fact, it was to be a mild, clear, and dry day. There would be no flight delays or cancellations. It was going to be a picture-perfect weekend. As he placed the laptop on the floor, a funny thought came to his mind. He never told Eva to pack a swim suit. If they were going to take the plunge in the lake, she surely needed one. When he called her to suggest that she bring one along, she told him that she figured they'd probably be taking a dip, so already added it to her checklist. The call wasn't wasted; for the couple continued to talk for another hour.

He laughed at himself at the thought of having asked her, *How long can you hold your breath underwater?* It didn't matter what her response would be for he had already phoned Lucci to ask that he have a pair of aqua lungs ready in the event that Eva would agree to join him. He could hear the excitement in Lucci's voice about the strong possibility that Seth would be returning with his possible mate. In the front of Seth's mind was Ariel. *Will she pop up especially since Eva is going to be there?* He wondered if she'd be jealous or would she be as welcoming to Eva as she was to him. Although he smiled as he imagined having to kiss Eva underwater as Ariel had done to him, he knew that the oxygen tanks would be sufficient.

Seth sat in bed, role-playing Eva's response to the secret of Mirror Lake, especially when he'd reveal that she has been dating "Adam Tiller," and that father and son is really one and the same person! *How doesn't something like that blow a person's mind?* The thought made him begin to worry. Another worry soon came to his mind. He didn't want to go to work tomorrow, so tossed and turned thinking of what he should do. Peale wouldn't be around, so it wouldn't cause a scene if Seth called in sick. Yet, he also wanted to clear his name for he didn't like being called an impostor, and for being accused of knocking off Adam Tiller. *What will happen if Eva rejects the idea of spending the rest of her life with me at Mirror Lake? I might very well have to return to Manhattan as Seth Tiller.* It prompted him to shoot an e-mail to Peale, as Adam Tiller. In this way the two accusations lodged against Seth would be proven as untruths. He picked up the laptop and wrote:

My dear Vincent,

I hope that all is well. The weather is absolutely gorgeous, and the book is coming along very well.

My son called me earlier today, and was upset that he had to lie to you and to me about his past. He was very contrite in explaining the situation to me. Please forgive him for not being honest. In light of the circumstances he did what he thought was right. I hold no grudges, and am more delighted that I have a son that I could call my own! I expect you to be just as forgiving, and make sure that he is given a better position with the company than the one you had chosen for him. I am still convinced that he has the potential to become a great writer based on the portfolio of his work that he left for me to read in between my own writing.

Be well, Vincent. You should consider taking some time off, too. You certainly deserve it, and speaking from my own experience; it could be the best thing you've ever done for yourself.

Sincerely,

Adam

As Seth pressed the send button, he knew the problem with Vincent Peale was alleviated, yet he had to cover all bases. Pretending he'd know nothing of his father's e-mail, Seth planned to stop by Peale's office on Monday and apologize for not telling him the truth. He'd confess that he wasn't sure how his dad would react, if he knew the truth about him. If he was aware of his difficult upbringing and lack of education, his father may not have accepted him. Going to Temple was only a fabrication to gain a higher status with his dad upon meeting him. Once he met his dad and hopefully be accepted with open arms, he'd tell him the truth. He would then say that due to his last encounter with Peale, Seth was forced to call his dad, and to discuss the situation. He would finally say that his father didn't care about his past or lack of education. He was just happy to have a son. So Peale wouldn't conclude that he was a "beach bum," Seth would purport that although he was never a college student, he left high school in his senior year to work as an auto mechanic.

Seth felt that it wasn't the greatest alibi, but it helped to resolve the issue regarding his lack of a college career. Hopefully, Peale wouldn't ask for whom he worked, or to one day look under the hood of his car! If Peale continued to cause any trouble, Adam Tiller would intervene, fire Peale, and find another publisher for his books; including his latest one, a sure best seller. Peale was too greedy a man to let some suspicion get in the way of adding to his fortune. He also knew that Tiller held the greatest portion of the company's stock, so becoming his enemy would lead to certain financial ruin. Seth was satisfied with his little scheme, and believed that he wouldn't have Peale to worry about any more. Now, he only had to focus on Eva, but there would be no deceit involved in this situation. He planned to be totally honest with her, and hoped that she would accept his invitation to join him forever at Mirror Lake.

Chapter Twenty-Three
Back to the Future

Seth awakened at five a.m., still unsure whether or not to call in sick. What if something came up, and Peale either never left or came back early? It would only raise more suspicion if he didn't go to work. Peale might round up the New York National Guard that would prevent Seth from escaping to Mirror Lake. He elected to take the safer course, and to put in at least a half day. He checked his e-mails to see if Peale had responded to his, but found nothing. He was glad that he opted to go to work for indeed, Peale was there.

As planned, he went directly to his office, and apologized to him for lying about attending Temple University. He confessed that he only made up the story to impress his father by telling him that he aspired to follow in his footsteps by attending his alma mater. When Peale asked how he could explain his writing ability, Seth said it must be in the genes, but also that he did take writing classes in high school that helped him to sharpen his writing skills. Peale appeared to be satisfied with his explanation. Seth was sure that the e-mail he sent last night was a determining factor in his change of heart. He asked no further questions, and although he wasn't certain if this was good or bad, at least it didn't seem that Peale was going to call in the police. He never said anything about receiving an e-mail from his dad. Perhaps the thought of the negative consequences of giving Seth a hard time was guiding his actions.

Seth said that he'd be leaving early from work. Peale countered by saying he was planning to do the same thing, and that he was still heading out for the convention although a day late. Seth returned to his cubicle, having expected to be transferred to another department. It seemed that Peale still wasn't sure what to do with him. It didn't matter any more to Seth for he felt the e-mail had resolved the problem, and there was a good chance that he wouldn't be returning on Monday. He also planned to call in sick on Friday for he had his fill of Tiller's Publishing House. Before he left at noon, he stopped by Marge Ritter's office to tell her that he wasn't returning after lunch. Although it wasn't his intention, the words seemed to flow from his tongue as if he was giving her a farewell address. When she approached to give him a big hug with teary eyes, his gut feeling was confirmed.

He spent a quiet evening at home, had a light dinner, and talked to Eva before retiring. On Friday morning, he spent a couple of hours jogging in Central Park, and relaxed all afternoon by reading the newest Lee Child novel. After he tidied up his apartment he showered, packed up, and waited for the airport van that promptly arrived to pick up Seth first, and then Eva. He called Lucci to have him stock up the fridge and food cupboard for the weekend, and planned to have something light to eat with Eva, once they arrived at the airport.

Eva was excited about going to Mirror Lake, and during their brief meal asked him to give her an idea of what she was going to experience. He spoke about the beautiful sunrise and sunset, the walk in the woods, fishing, Storm, the loons and finally the peace and quiet it afforded. He said nothing about its secret. Eva admitted that she had very little camping experience and that she wasn't too fond of bugs, yet she was looking forward to the weekend in the wilderness. Seth assured her that she was in for a real treat. She was glad to hear that they were sleeping in a warm cozy log cabin, rather than in a tent that needed to be pitched, and suspect to leaks and all sorts of creepy crawlers.

Seth asked what Eva's mother said when she called earlier in the evening. Eva answered by telling Seth that she thought it was a good idea to get away, especially since she was under a lot of stress due to the lack of employment prospects. She also mentioned how much she liked and trusted Seth, who would be nothing less than the perfect gentleman. He was surprised to hear that Mrs. LoPresti told Eva that she wasn't expecting to hear from her over the weekend. Eva shared that she was raised to be an independent woman, and that her mother wasn't the kind who demanded her daughter to text or call her every day. It was Eva who chose to visit every weekend, and not that it was expected by her mother. Mrs. LoPresti seemed to be gradually letting go of any maternal reins, especially after she was diagnosed with ovarian cancer, and in the hope of preparing Eva for her passing from this life. Seth was glad to be hearing this for Eva's sake, as well as in light of what he'd be asking of her by tomorrow.

Seth planned to show Eva the underwater world first, and then explain how he fit into it, and of course Eva. He expected that she was going to be as dumbfounded as he was when he first saw it. He would then have to tell her who he really is. He imagined that this would be a hard pill for her to swallow. Once the secret was revealed, and Seth would vocalize how he thought Eva could possibly fit in, the rest would be up to her. Would she choose to join him in this paradise as the new Eve? He knew that she was going to be overwhelmed by his revelation, and that a favorable decision wouldn't come easily. He recalled how long it took him to process all the implausible information, so he had to expect that Eva wasn't going to make a facile decision. He had to be prepared for a negative reaction to what she'd see and hear, and be ready to leave Mirror Lake in an instant, if she so desired.

As Eva fell asleep on the plane approaching Green Bay, Seth theorized how he'd respond should Eva give him a definite, "NO," for an answer. Was there someone else out there who would agree to join him? Perhaps he'd end up replacing Lucci as the guardian of the secret, until someone like himself came along. Living alone in a log cabin wasn't as glamorous as living with Eva in a new world. He didn't think that returning to Manhattan to slave at the publishing house as a copy-editor was the answer. Sooner or later, when Adam Tiller wasn't around to protect him, Peale's suspicion would resurface, and Seth would be confronting another round of trouble. It was obvious that his only option was to remain at Mirror Lake, whether it was with Eva or not.

The only bad feature of having a night flight was that the couple had to take the mile walk from the main road to the cabin in total darkness. Thankfully, Lucci picked them up at the airport, and provided them with powerful flashlights. Seeing Eva, Lucci volunteered to carry her bags. Seth saw in his eyes that he was captivated by her beauty. Seth was pleased by the excitement that the walk in the woods generated in Eva, and hoped that it was a good omen for what was to come. Seth was charmed by Eva's unique giggle, and the fact that she was giggling throughout the walk, gave him a sense that she was going to like it here. She was buoyant as two deer ran across the path only a few feet in front of them. Seth reminded her of Storm, and wondered if the fawn would pay them a visit over the weekend knowing that he was back. Eva expressed her hope that it would make an appearance saying, "It would be really cool to have it feed off my hand, and to pet it as I would a dog or a cat."

Lucci left a light on in the cabin when he dropped off the groceries and scuba gear earlier in the day. As they approached the cabin, Eva voiced how impressed she was by the ruggedness of the shanty, and that it wasn't as she had expected. Seth pointed the beam of light to the tree where the loon had nested, but there was no evidence of its presence. He then, showed Eva the dock where the small row boat was moored. The light traveled from the dock down the channel to the main body of the lake, and was met by the light of the moon that lit up the lake, even though it was half its full size.

Seth asked Lucci if he'd like to stay awhile for something to drink, but he said that he had to return home. Seth knew that Lucci wanted to leave because he wanted the couple to settle in, and get down to the business of coming to Mirror Lake. Eva thanked him for carrying her luggage, and as he stood near Seth far enough from Eva so she couldn't hear, he whispered, "You have quite a catch here! Good luck." The two men exchanged smiles and shook hands. Seth reminded Lucci of their early flight on Sunday, and set up a time for pick up. Seth could always depend on him, and was grateful for all he had done. He thought for a moment being in Lucci's position as he stood by the door watching him start up the path. He concluded that he'd be just as accommodating, yet it didn't take away the admiration and appreciation he felt for the man.

Seth gave his guest a grand tour of both inside and outside of the cabin. She loved it, although she exclaimed that she could do without the ferocious black bear! It came time to set up their sleeping arrangements. Up until this point, the couple never ventured further into their relationship than experiencing a passionate kiss, nor ever spoke about how intimate they wanted to be. Seth recalled what Mrs. LoPresti said of him, being the perfect gentleman, and respected Eva's convictions as a Catholic, who had recently returned to a more active participation in her church. Given a second chance in life, Seth wanted to do things right. He placed her luggage in the room with the twin beds, and told her that this was where she was sleeping. She seemed to be fine with the decision he had made for her, although she'd be lying if she said she hadn't thought of wanting to share the same bed with him. The couple still exhilarated about spending the weekend together, unpacked their bags and met a few minutes later in the kitchen.

The loon clock displayed that it was three o'clock in the morning, yet neither of them was hungry or tired. Together they looked to see what was in the fridge and food pantry, and chatted about what they would put together for meals throughout the weekend. Seth started a fire and the pair nestled comfortably on the sofa. Normally, the time would be ripe to uncork a bottle of wine, but neither were drinkers. He put his arm around Eva's back. She followed his gesture by placing her head on his shoulder. Seth felt uneasy because he wanted to kiss Eva, and let his passion lead him to wherever it wanted to go; however, he respected Eva too much to do that. He tried to imagine what Eva was thinking, as he sat listening to the beat of both their hearts that made him recall the 1967 hit by Tommy James and the Shondells called *I Think We're Alone Now*. Seth enjoyed this newly-found closeness to Eva and the silence of their first night together, knowing that their nearest neighbors were the Native Americans, who lived on a reservation five miles away.

When Eva told him that she was thirsty, Seth brought her a glass of iced tea with a twist of lemon. Instead of sitting on the sofa, they chose to sit on the floor with their backs against the sofa, so to be closer to the fire. Eva told Seth that she already was fond of Mirror Lake to which he replied, "You haven't seen anything yet!" She also confessed that she would love being anywhere with him. *Even in an underwater paradise?* She told him how much he meant to her, as she had first announced at dinner the last time they were together. She repeated how much her mother liked

Seth, and how she had a feeling that they were meant for each other.

Seth moved his fingers through Eva's thick brown hair, and gave her a kiss on the side of the forehead. Once again, he shared his feelings about her, including his desire to spend the rest of his life with her. It was much more than a cliché, for he truly meant it in every sense of the word. She surprised Seth by asking why he had taken her to a place so far removed from home when there were other places closer to New York; and just as nice. He never perceived about how odd bringing Eva to Mirror Lake actually was, but knew that when its secret would finally be revealed tomorrow; she'd fully understand. For now, he answered her question by saying that he'd rather show her than to tell her. When he glanced at his wrist watch, he saw that it would soon be dawn, and that he planned on taking her on the lake to watch the sunrise. Seth suggested that since they had to get up in just a few hours that it would be a good idea to retire for the night. Eva agreed, but suggested that they sleep right where they were. Seth didn't lodge any protest.

Eva rose to her knees telling him that she loved him, and kissed him gently on the lips. In response, Seth rose to his knees while holding her kiss, and began to pass his fingers through her hair. Their gentle caresses became more passionate as their bodies rubbed against each other. They eased themselves to the floor and moved closer together. They explored each other's body tenderly with their hands; reaching a level of love-making that had not been previously realized.

Seth sat up against the sofa, and Eva placed her head on his thigh as she continued to lie on the floor. Both faced the fireplace, and watched the flames dance colorfully from one log to another. Seth reveled in this activity more than he did when he was by himself. He recalled the Scriptural passage from Genesis that was read during Mass at Saint Patrick's Cathedral when God said as he looked at Adam, "It is not good for the man to be alone." Seth gently stroked Eva's head, as she closed her eyes with pleasure and fell asleep in no more than two minutes with a smile on her face. Seth never before felt such oneness with another human being, and was engulfed in a moment that he did not want to end.

Seth didn't want to join his angel in sleep and miss the sunrise, so he set the alarm on his watch for five a.m. He thought for a few minutes of what tomorrow might bring, and tried to envision the expression on Eva's face, when she'd see the treasure of Mirror Lake. His side was bursting with joyful anticipation, and felt confident that she would accept the story that accompanied it; not only that Seth was really Adam Tiller, but that they were destined to live together as the new Adam and the new Eve. He not only believed it, but felt it in his innermost being. As Eva's mother said herself, they were meant for each other. Even though he felt good about what was going to happen tomorrow, he still would be ready for the worse. Judging how things had been going over the last few hours, the worse couldn't possibly be all that bad.

Chapter Twenty-Four

The Secret Revealed

As Seth heard the beeping of his watch alarm, it didn't seem that he had ever fallen asleep. He saw that Eva's head was still on his lap, and that she was sleeping undisturbed. After giving her a gentle nudge, she opened her eyes and smiled at him. While Eva freshened up, Seth gathered a few snacks and bottled water for their trip to the lake. There was a slight chill in the air, so both wore a sweat suit. Eva seemed a bit nervous as she boarded the bark, and confessed that she hadn't ever been on a small boat before. Seth slowly rowed up the channel, and into the main body of the lake. His timing was perfect for as the skiff reached the middle of the lake, the dawn was upon them with the start of a sensational sunrise. Eva's eyes glowed with sheer delight, as she watched and savored every second of the spectacle. They lay on the floor of the boat looking into the sky, wrapped in each other's arms, and seemingly unbothered by their close quarters. They were able to sneak in a few kisses and before long were sound asleep.

The light from the sun's climb to a higher position in the sky was what eventually awakened them. Eva marveled at the lake's beauty and as she looked into the water, understood how it received its name. Seth decided to row closer to the shore, and continued to steer the vessel along the bank. Eva was thrilled by the sight and sound of fish jumping in and out of the water, and was entertained by the diving birds having their morning snack. After Seth anchored the boat, they had a bite to eat and drank a bottle of water. Neither wanted to eat too much for they would rather enjoy the hearty breakfast at the cabin that they had spoken about earlier. There was no talking albatross, mermaid, or gentle behemoth to welcome Eva to Mirror Lake, and it suited Seth just fine.

Upon their return to the cabin, they sat on the porch and chatted for a few minutes before Seth rose to get a few carrots in the event that Storm might pay them a visit. The couple was not to be disappointed for the fawn soon arrived, as if it had smelled the carrots from wherever it was foraging. Eva was delighted that the deer not only ate off her hand, but allowed her to pet it. Seth hoped that the loons would also make an appearance, but it wasn't going to be the case at least for the moment.

Seth showed Eva the outside shower, and invited her to shower first. He was relieved that she wasn't concerned by the lack of hot water. He did suggest using the bath tub and offered to heat water, but she didn't want him to go through the trouble. As she bathed, Seth fried bacon and when she returned to the kitchen, Seth left for his turn to take his shower while Eva peeled white potatoes for the home-fries. Later, they diced veggies and Eva made a wicked western omelet. Both drank orange juice, yet Seth still brewed a fresh pot of coffee for Eva. In time, he'd talk to her about cutting out the caffeine. As the couple enjoyed their meal, Seth imagined what it would be like having Eva around the house. She was absolutely gorgeous, even with her hair tied up and hidden under a bath towel. She needed no cosmetics for she possessed a natural beauty that he had never seen in a woman before. At one time, Eva caught Seth staring at her, so she asked, "What?" He only smiled and replied, "Oh, nothing; it's just that you're so beautiful."

Seth knew that Eva had packed a swim suit, yet never asked if she could swim. Chances were that a girl, who never boarded a row boat, had never learned how to swim. If she couldn't swim, the thought of wearing an aqua lung and swimming underwater must have totally worried her. After he found the strength to ask, he was relieved to hear that she was a good swimmer, and very excited about swimming underwater. She asked Seth if this had anything to do with why he brought her to Mirror Lake. Smiling he responded, "It had *everything* to do with it!" That was as much as he wanted to say about it, and from the way Eva looked, it seemed as if she was expecting something on which she had never laid eyes. She had that right!

After cleaning up, they readied themselves for the first leg of their adventure—the walk through the woods. Seth took a couple bottles of water, and found a hiking stick for both of them while waiting for Eva. Although she had never hiked through the woods before, she enjoyed the hour and a half walk. When they returned to the cabin, Eva rested on the porch sipping on an iced tea, and feeding Storm sliced apples. Seth prepared lunch, and placed all the fishing and scuba gear on the boat. He felt himself getting giddier than nervous, as the secret of Mirror Lake was soon to be revealed. As they rowed out, Seth told her that they would probably be on the lake all afternoon, and cap off the experience watching the sunset. Eva was excited, and had no reservations about spending the entire day on Mirror Lake, especially since it would be spent with Seth.

Seth took out a tube of sun screen, and suggested that Eva apply it on her body, knowing how scorching the sun's rays could be on the lake. Eva was well-toned, and her skin was as soft as silk. It pleased him when she asked that he assist her by putting some lotion on her back and shoulders. As his hands slid smoothly across her body, a feeling of warmth passed through him; not the warmth generated by the sun for this feeling came from within him. It became an opportunity for them to enjoy another round of kisses. Even though Seth didn't think he needed any protection from the ultra-violet rays of the sun due to his deep dark tan, he didn't resist when Eva offered to rub him with the lotion. She removed his t-shirt, and took delight in applying it on his shoulders and back. He didn't stop her when she asked him to turn around, and proceeded to cover his chest with another dab of lotion. Seth being very much caught up in the sensuality of her action could not resist kissing her more passionately. The sudden splash of a diving bird only a few feet from the boat, shook Seth out of his ecstasy, and moved his thoughts in another direction.

Eva surprised Seth, when she asked if she could row the boat. After carefully switching positions, she put the oars into the water, and as she started off began to splash Seth. Neither could stop laughing. Seth explained how to *feather* the oars to prevent splashing. Eva caught on quickly, and after mastering the rowing method to perfection, had the skiff gliding gracefully across the water. When Seth figured they had gone far enough into the lake, he asked Eva to stop, and anchored the boat. He had baited the two fishing lines with artificial lures as Eva was rowing, so was now ready to give her a lesson in casting. Just as she had caught on with rowing, she did the same when it came to casting her line. Seth was impressed by her first cast that traveled thirty feet from the boat. As had happened many times with Seth, the bait received an immediate hit the second it struck the water. He told her to give the line a jerk, and then to start reeling it in.

Seth didn't know whether he or Eva was having the most enjoyable time, as the catch came closer to the boat, giving Eva a decent fight. Instructing her to stay low in the boat, he took the hand net, and helped to pull the fish out of the water. As it wiggled in the net, the fish splashed water on both of them that brought more laughs. Eva would have no part in unhooking the fish, so Seth had to do the honor. He told her that she had snagged an eighteen inch pickerel. Eva was so thrilled, and could hardly wait to cast again. Not concentrating as carefully as she should, she forgot to release her thumb from the button of her Zebco at the appropriate time, thus resulting in a cast that hit the side of the boat, and landed an inch away from Seth's leg! Although it could have been a disaster for Seth, he started to laugh. When Eva saw that Seth wasn't mad, but humored by it, she also joined him in a hearty laugh. Seth couldn't recall the last time he had so much fun with another person.

Within the hour and a half of fishing, the two anglers pulled in over twenty fish. They were also starting to feel the heat of the sun on their back and shoulders, as well as the discomfort of the rising temperature. It was time to take the plunge. Seth asked if she wanted to take an underwater swim. He could sense her apprehension, even though she was all for it a few hours ago. He congratulated her for being such a great fisherman, and for learning, so quickly, the art of rowing. She graciously attributed her success to Seth's expert coaching. He convinced her that she would find this next adventure, as easy as it was to learn rowing and casting. At least Seth hoped she would; never having had the experience himself.

Seth removed the lures from the fishing lines, and put the rods aside. He pulled up the anchor, and rowed to the spot he guessed was near the underwater cavern. When they arrived at their destination, the couple prepared to put on their scuba gear. Although he had never gone scuba diving, Seth pretended to know what he was doing; to allay any fear Eva may have had. He gave her a mini-lesson, as best he could fabricate, and helped her to place the single tank on her back. After putting on their mask and a set of fins they were good to go. Seth told her what to expect underwater, and to stay close to him. Sounding as if he knew what he was talking about, he told Eva that divers usually fall backwards into the water from a sitting position, but it would be fine to climb out of the boat one leg at a time, and simply sink into the lake. He turned on both their oxygen tanks and asked Eva to give him a "thumbs up," once she felt the oxygen enter her lungs. After giving him the signal, he helped her into the water. He thought for a moment to try diving in backwards, as he'd seen in the movies, but since Eva made it look easy enough, he chose to take the plunge the safer way. Besides, he didn't want to embarrass himself, the expert that he had feigned to be!

Eva was astonished by the clarity of the water, and of how far she could see in all directions. She kicked her feet as Seth had instructed, and was pleased by how easy it was to swim underwater. The fins made a big difference. Eva swam close to Seth, and together reveled in the sight of the lake's marine life. She pointed excitedly to a school of colorful fish, and was delighted when she spied a large turtle swim by them.

Seth recalled the first time he had taken the plunge, and how Ariel had to twice fill his lungs with oxygen in order to reach the cavern. He smiled at the thought of giving Eva an underwater kiss, but knew that he'd never want to chance it. As the duo approached their destination, Seth was relieved that neither the mermaid nor behemoth had showed; for they would have certainly scared Eva to death! He could feel the rush of adrenalin, as they neared the entrance of Mirror Lake's great treasure. Eva was in for the shock of her life. Seth was the first to get out of the water, and then turned to help Eva. She excitedly spoke about what she had seen underwater, and was obviously enraptured by it. Seth tried to prepare her for what would come next. He told her that this was the reason for bringing her to Mirror Lake. He confessed that he had discovered this wondrous place, while he was here a couple of weeks ago, and that he and Lucci were the only two people who know that it exists. Eva may have been expecting to see a large cave with colorful and unusual rock formations, perhaps even a number of bats; but never in her wildest imagination, would she have imagined the world that lay before her.

Seth removed his aqua lung and underwater mask, but left on his fins. He told Eva to do the same. He knew that there was some rocky terrain to cross before they entered the portal, so it would be easier on their feet. As they approached the threshold from their world to one that was full of mystery, they slipped out of their fins, held hands, and entered. Eva's eyes widened with bewilderment, as she took in her first glimpse of the marvelous place. She looked around her, and then stared back at Seth in disbelief. They walked in silence for a few minutes before she asked Seth, "What is this beautiful place?" He responded by using a single word—"Paradise!"

They continued to walk as if in a daze; mesmerized by what they saw, heard, smelled and touched. The only sense they didn't test was that of taste. Who could blame them; not knowing whether something was poisonous or edible? They walked for over an hour, and passed where Seth had ventured the last time he was there. At a short distance from this mark, the couple came to a beautiful waterfall that gave off a mist helping to form a rainbow, as the falling water noisily splashed into the pool at the bottom. Eva was awed by its beauty, saying that it was a sight that she had only seen on a postcard. They walked into the pool of water until waist high, and enjoyed the spectacle as up close and natural as possible. Seth looked at Eva whose face and hair was so enhanced by the mist; making her appear as if she was a water nymph. For a few minutes, they swam in the enchanted pool as if they were two lovers from an ancient Greek myth.

After taking in this most remarkable experience for nearly a half hour, they emerged from the water, and sat on a large rock. Eva had a number of questions that Seth weakly answered, or could not answer all. When she had exhausted all she could possibly ask, the stage was set to reveal the rest of Mirror Lake's secret. He began by talking about Lucci and his son; that Lucci was the guardian of this wonderful place, and that he wanted to pass the baton to him. She couldn't understand why Lucci wanted out, or why Seth would even consider being his replacement. He knew that it was time to tell her who he really was. To Seth, it was the perfect setting for which he desired, and he believed that its timing was right. He hoped that the mist that had engulfed his beloved Eva, would somehow cast a magical spell of acceptance upon her.

Seth started again with Lucci, the young man she met last night, who was really quite older than he looked. He explained that he is the *father* of a son, who had died recently. This son of his was over seventy years of age! He told Eva how the waters of the lake caused an age regression in Lucci. She was flabbergasted by what she was hearing, and at one point shook her head and said, "Say that again." It was incomprehensible to believe, but it would only get worse.

The next part of the story was the hardest for Seth to tell and the most arduous for Eva to process. He began by telling her that he was the famous writer, Adam Tiller, and that there is really no Seth. He told her about why he came to Mirror Lake, the mermaid, gentle behemoth, and how the water gradually changed him from a man of sixty-three into one forty years younger. Eva asked no further questions, nor did she make any comments throughout Seth's explanation. When he finished, he held his breath and waited for her response.

Eva sat in a state of shock for a brief moment. His gut instincts told him that she didn't take his story very well, and that she would soon spring up, dart out of the cavern, and ask to be taken home immediately! Could he really blame her? He broke the uncomfortable silence to express what would be even more disconcerting for Eva to hear. He began to share his view of why he had to stumble upon this enchanting place, and what he believed was Eva's connection. As Seth expected, it was just too much for Eva to process. She didn't wait to hear Seth's spiel about the couple becoming the new Adam and the new Eve, and both destined to live in the new Eden, as the first parents of a fully-redeemed humanity. She abruptly rose from the rock, and began walking back to the entrance of the cavern. Seth followed behind her, and neither said a single word to each other during the entire time. Apparently, he had Eva all wrong.

Chapter Twenty-Five

The Choice

When the pair came to the entrance of the cavern, they slipped into their fins, and Eva allowed Seth to help strap on her aqua lung. Together, they swam back to the boat. Seth climbed in first, and then helped Eva. He took the oars, and began to row back to the cabin. Eva was seated with her back toward him, and didn't say a single word until they stood on the porch; when she asked, "Am I going to show any age regression?" Although Seth was surprised by her question, at least he knew that she believed his story. He told her that he didn't know, but it was unlikely. She wasn't very happy that he didn't have all the facts, and couldn't fathom how he could have placed her in such jeopardy. Seth never thought about the possibility of Eva also experiencing age regression for in his eyes; she was the closest person he had ever met to perfection.

For the first time since the couple met, Seth was scared to death; first, for the possibility that she could wake up tomorrow as a teenager, and second, that she might decide never to speak to him again. He couldn't choose what would be worse. Eva proceeded to her room, and closed the door behind her. After waiting a half hour for her to come out, he opted to take a shower. When he returned to the cabin, he saw that her door was still closed, so he went to his room to change into something casual. While dressing, he chose to knock at Eva's door to reach out to her, but as he approached her bedroom, he saw that her door was now open and that she was showering. Seth walked onto the porch, and sat somberly on the rocking chair; blaming himself for having made a dreadful mistake. He should have told her about the secret instead of letting her see it. He hated to hurt her, and for putting her into a dangerous situation. He wished that he had never come to Mirror Lake, nor had met Eva LoPresti. The family of loons wobbled from the channel and approached, as if looking for something to eat. Seth tried to smile as he said, "Well, look, who finally arrived." He was in no mood to feed them, nor did he really care much about them. All he cared about was Eva. He thought that it would be best that she return to the city without him; feeling that he had no other choice than to remain at Mirror Lake to protect its secret. As beautiful and promising as it once was, it was now nothing but a prison and a curse to him.

Seth must have sat for nearly a half hour, engulfed in his thoughts before Eva came out and stood before him. She wore a red robe, and had a bath towel around her head. To Seth, she was just as beautiful as ever. He stood up, but before he could say anything, Eva put her finger on his lips. She said that she wanted to go back on the lake to watch the sunset. He thought that it was a strange request in light of the circumstances, but at the same time it provided a glimmer of hope.

It would be a couple of hours to sunset, so in the interim the couple prepared dinner that included, veal Marsala with angel hair pasta and fresh asparagus. Eva couldn't believe that Lucci would go out of his way to provide such a meal. As Seth worked on the main course, Eva prepared a spinach salad, topped with luscious strawberries and almonds. Seth warmed a small loaf of Italian bread. He couldn't help to think that the addition of a fine bottle of white wine would make a perfect dinner; however, he knew that it was best for both of them to settle for a pitcher of iced tea with lemon.

The couple worked silently as they prepared dinner, and finally sat at table to eat what was hardly the romantic dinner that Seth had planned. It was an uncomfortable setting, and different from all the meals they shared before that was characterized by laughter, romance, and good feelings. Seth suggested they eat dessert and clean up after they returned from the lake; for it was getting close to sunset. Eva nodded, said that she was going to freshen up, and that she'd be ready in a few minutes. Seth waited for Eva on the porch, while feeding bread morsels to the loons. Eva was delighted to see Seth's feathered-friends and after feeding them herself, the couple made their way to the dock.

Seth rowed onto the lake, and chose to stay close to the cabin. Unlike the poor timing in the revealing of Mirror Lake's secret earlier in the afternoon; his timing to view the sunset was perfect, and more beautiful than Eva had ever imagined. She sat on the seat with her back, once again, facing Seth. The exhilaration she felt as she watched the sky explode into color, moved her to turn to Seth and say, "This is the most breath-taking thing that I have ever experienced! Why haven't I ever noticed how spectacular the daily event of the sun's rising and setting truly is?" Seth knew the feeling and replied, "Because in life, we often miss the most important things. Pursuing fame, fortune and other material things, our selfishness, and wanting to satisfy our sensual appetite, keep us from seeing them. Coming to Mirror Lake has helped me to appreciate the simple, yet wonderful pleasures of life such as the rising and setting of the sun."

Eva smiled faintly and turned back around. It wasn't time to cuddle with Seth, or to pretend that everything was fine between them. She gazed with wonder and awe into the sky, perplexed by what to do after hearing the astonishing story that Seth had shared. She needed God's help, now more than ever. *Dear Lord, what am I to do?* She wanted a clear, immediate, and direct answer. She envisioned Him riding in a fiery chariot across the heavens and stopping to reveal the answer; however, she knew that God didn't usually work that way. More often than not, His will is revealed more subtly through nature, people, or the daily events in life. It suddenly dawned on Eva that He may have already answered her in coming to Mirror Lake. She had to let go and let God. She had to trust what her heart was telling her, even though her mind couldn't fully understand all she had seen and heard.

Seth realized that Eva was trying to process his story, and that she needed the time to arrive at a decision. Just as the lake provided for him; he sensed that it was now working on her. After waiting for what seemed to be an eternity, Eva turned to Seth with teary eyes and began to speak. She first apologized to him for her behavior. She told him how uncomfortable it was to give him the silent treatment in the cavern and throughout dinner. She told him that his story was too difficult to comprehend and was best to say nothing; rather than something that she might later regret. She gave no indication whether she wanted to stay at the cabin or be taken to some hotel until the flight.

After finishing what she had to say, Seth responded by first apologizing to her for not telling her the truth before taking her to Mirror Lake. He shared his own struggle with how to convey this remarkable story to her. He admitted that he used poor judgment in showing, rather than, telling her about Mirror Lake. Eva appreciated his candor, agreed that it was a hard call to make, and that neither were perfect ways to reveal such a remarkable secret.

Eva picked up the conversation by asking a number of questions that Seth answered as best he could. He voiced his own difficulty in coming to grips; not only with what he saw here, but to find the meaning in all of it. At this time, he was able to communicate his idea of being a new Adam in search of the new Eve, and how he came to the conclusion that she was the woman of his destiny. He conceded that it is an outlandish idea, and begged her forgiveness if he was out of line in considering her. He put the proverbial ball in her court when he asked, "What do you think about this place and our future here?" Eva said that she wasn't sure at this point, and needed more time to think it over. Once again, Seth could appreciate her reservation for he had already gone through the same experience.

By now, another sunset had become history, and darkness replaced the color show in the sky. The couple felt a slight chill in the air, and noticed that a thin fog was forming over the lake. Seth suggested that they return to the cabin that could be seen at a distance, since he left a light on. He told Eva that they still had dessert to eat, and if she wanted, they could continue their conversation. As he rowed back to his hovel, the idea of the cabin as a symbol of hope returned to his mind. He knew that what would go on there over the next few hours, could determine the outcome of both his and Eva's future. He had to tread carefully, and avoid saying anything that would make matters worse.

Once inside, Seth made a half pot of coffee, and the two sat at the kitchen table eager to continue their discussion. Eva brought up what had been in the front of his mind, namely, her mother. As expected, she voiced her apprehension at the thought of leaving her dying mother; even if she could somehow consent to be part of Seth's phenomenal proposition. Seth said that he could empathize with her, and understood that it was too much to ask. In fact, he insisted that her place was at home by her mother's side; even should Mrs. LoPresti try to persuade her to return to him.

Seth served vanilla ice cream on pound cake topped with strawberries. He sipped on a second glass of iced tea, as Eva drank a cup of fresh coffee. When they finished, the couple cleaned up, including what had been left at lunch and made their way into the living room. After striking up a small fire, Seth sat next to Eva on the sofa and the couple continued to talk about Mirror Lake. After all that had possibly been said by both parties, Eva paused for a brief moment, and revealed that she had arrived at her final decision. Eva chose to return home to tend to her sick mother. She had no idea how long it would take, but it would give her the time to think about their future as well. She exhorted him to refrain from calling her, but promised that she wouldn't desert him. Seth thought that it was a decision with which he could live, especially having concluded earlier that everything was over between them. With hope, he could live for another day.

Coming to the realization that there was nothing else to talk about, and not wanting to become intimate with Seth; Eva stood up. She gave him a peck on the cheek, and said that she was going to bed. Seth wanted her to stay, but knew that she needed both the time and space. Before retiring himself, he approached Eva's room seeing that she kept the door open. Peeking in, he saw that she was already asleep. The moon was shedding its light through the window, and fell radiantly upon her face. It made Eva look as if she was an angel. A tear came to his eye as he thought of the grief that he brought her, and worse, imagined what his life would be without her.

As he lie in bed, Seth recalled all that had transpired throughout the day, and that his life with Eva might soon be coming to an end; nonetheless, he was relieved that he had been able to finally get Mirror Lake off his chest. He realized that Eva's reaction could have been far worse.

At present, she was still with him, they were talking and there was a chance, albeit a slim one, that they could end up together. He wasn't sure whether or not it would be at Mirror Lake for that was now left in her hands to decide. He recited a brief prayer, asking God for the patience he needed in the weeks or months ahead. The last image in his mind before falling asleep was Jesus in the Garden of Gethsemane on the night before he died, while praying to His Heavenly Father. He, too, struggled with making an important decision that involved mankind's *first* redemption. Seth's words tonight, were the same as those of Jesus, *Not my will, but yours be done.*

Seth forgot to type an entry in his journal, and also to set his alarm. At eight a.m. he felt a gentle nudge. Eva stood beside his bed looking down and smiling, as she did before going to the underwater cavern. She announced that breakfast was now being served. After freshening up, Seth joined Eva in the kitchen, and the first thing he did was to walk up to her and kiss her on the cheek saying, "I owe you one." He apologized for sleeping in, and not helping her with the meal. Eva shrugged it off, and said that it was a way of thanking him for all he did yesterday. Breakfast was followed by the couple sitting on the porch to take in the dawn of another beautiful day at Mirror Lake. Eva had already sliced an apple, and hoped that Storm would make an appearance. She was not disappointed for the little fawn fearlessly walked up to them within a few minutes. Seth told her that he was convinced that Storm watched every move he made. Eva nodded, and took delight in feeding the deer and petting its soft pelt.

Having fed Storm, Eva asked if Seth noticed any age regression in her. Seth hadn't given it much thought since they spoke about it yesterday, and was jubilant when he saw that none had taken place. He explained that the same thing happened to Lucci, yet he was the only member of the family that had experienced it. Again, it remained another mystery of the lake, and along with Eva was baffled how the lake seemed to choose who changed, and who didn't. It was an eerie thought. Seth did share what Lucci had speculated about why his son hadn't experienced age regression, yet Eva couldn't agree that she was in no need of redemption. Seth saw otherwise, for to him, Eva was the most innocent, pure and selfless person that he had ever met.

They didn't have to meet Lucci for another couple of hours, so Seth asked if Eva would join him for another walk through the woods. Eva accepted his invitation, and after putting on more appropriate clothing; the couple set out. They didn't stray far from the cabin, yet still had an exhilarating hike. Upon returning to the cabin they took showers, and packed up for the flight back home. Seth knew that Eva hadn't written him off, and that there was a chance that she'd choose to join him at Mirror Lake once her mother would be laid to rest. When it was time, they made their way to the road where Lucci was waiting. He told Lucci that only Eva was returning to Manhattan. Lucci told Seth to take Eva to the airport, and that he'd be waiting in the cabin.

Before leaving, Eva thanked Lucci for his kindness, and that it was a pleasure having met him. She also told him that he was a very brave man, and gave him a hug and a kiss on the cheek. Lucci wished her the best, and after putting her luggage in the trunk, started out for the cabin. Seth was able to point out the Indian reservation that Eva was not able to see on Friday night, as well as other scenic views that were reminiscent of the northwoods of Wisconsin.

When they arrived at the airport terminal, Seth approached the desk attendant, and said that only Eva was boarding the plane. Together they checked in Eva's luggage, and waited until it was time to depart. As the call was made over the PA system, both rose to their feet and hugged. This time they kissed each other on their lips. Seth told Eva to give her mom, "a big Hello," and promised to keep them both in his thoughts and prayers. Before Eva walked out of his sight, she turned back to wave and throw a kiss. Seth returned it with one of his own and a final wave. He didn't envy what lay ahead of her, and trusted that she would one day get back to him. Yet, wondered if he'd ever see her again.

Chapter Twenty-Six

The End or a New Beginning

On the way back to the cabin Seth passed a tavern, and for a brief moment was tempted to pull over and drown the sorrow he felt in Eva's departure with booze; nevertheless, he knew that it wouldn't bring her back. He had been down that path before, and was not going to let alcohol destroy Seth Tiller. Besides, he knew that Lucci was waiting for him at the cabin. He found his friend sitting on the porch with Storm at his feet. The sight brought a smile to his face, as it looked to be more a dog than a deer. He bent down and rubbed the fawn behind its ears, and sat on the floor with his back against one of the wooden posts. He told Lucci where things stood, and asked if he could renew the lease. Lucci said that there was no reason to sign a lease, and that he could remain at the cabin for as long as necessary. Seth invited him for dinner, but Lucci said that he had to be on his way. Seth thanked him for his kindness and patience, and promised to call him once he heard from Eva. He told Seth that he'd continue to pick up his grocery list, and purchase anything else he desired. Storm rose with Lucci, and walked along side him up the trail as if it was truly "man's best friend."

Before doing anything else, Seth took out his laptop to catch up with his journal writing. The entry for today was the most hellacious one that he had to write. He stopped a few times to wipe away his tears. At one point, he had to get up and take a walk to clear the lump in his throat. Thus began, the most torturous time of his life. *Will Eva ever return? Will I ever see her again?* Seth found some leftovers to eat in the fridge, and was in bed by nine o'clock. He didn't do any reading for he wanted to meet his beloved in his dreams. His cell phone rang sometime during the night, or perhaps in the early morning. It was Eva who called to say that she arrived safely at LaGuardia, and was now home. There was one more thing she had to say that would plant a seed of hope in him. She told him that she loved him. He replied, "And I love you, too."

The next morning he woke at six, and returned to his daily regimen of hiking, fishing, reading, and journaling. He walked along the river, and spent the entire day in the woods. He began to bring his laptop with him, and would sit under a tree or on a rock, adding material to his journal. In time, he had enough to fill a book of seven hundred pages, yet, had no idea of how he was going to end the book. Eva would help him to write it, once he had heard of her decision.

He thought of Eva morning, noon, and night. He prayed for Mrs. LoPresti, and wondered if she would have much pain especially in her last days. *Will she experience a peaceful death? How will Eva respond to her suffering and death?* All he could do was to hope and pray. On the day after Eva left, Seth started to tie up a few loose ends. First, he set up an account at a local bank, and had a substantial amount of money wired to it. He didn't care about other assets such as his properties, financial portfolio, and the publishing house. His accountant was given more responsibility, and his lawyer would handle the estate. In the event of his death, all of his fortune would be left to his son, Seth Tiller. No matter what Eva would tell him, he decided that he'd never return to the city or his former way of life.

He had to sever his relationship with Vincent Peale, so he penned a letter as Seth Tiller to inform him that working at Tiller's Publishing House wasn't what he wanted to do in life, and that he returned to live with his mother in Ohio. He grinned at the thought of Peale trying to track him down, going through one town after another asking for a man who didn't exist!

He also had to deal a death blow to Peale, so as Adam Tiller sent an e-mail telling that he knew all along about the affair between his wife and him. He finally found the courage to tell him exactly how he felt, and that he was looking for a new publisher. It brought great delight when he typed the words, "You're fired!" He was at peace with his decision of never returning to the Big Apple. He found a much smaller apple that turned out to be far more appealing. He knew that Peale had no clue where he was, so had no fear of being hunted down by him.

He closed the laptop, and smiled with great satisfaction. He had only one more loose end; namely, who would he choose to live as—Adam or Seth Tiller? Before he could make this decision he needed to hear from Eva. As the days passed into weeks and the weeks into months, Tiller sat on the sofa or porch, the recliner or boat, playing out in his mind, how he would live as either man, and how he'd do away with them. He foresaw a life that could be lived happily as either, but above all, he hoped that it would be with Eva. It didn't matter where he'd live, even if it wasn't at Mirror Lake; as long as it was with Eva. In the passing of time, it became crystal clear to him—If Eva wasn't going to be a part of his future, then he'd live the rest of his life at Mirror Lake.

Lucci stopped by to pay him a visit one morning. The couple sat on the porch for two hours sipping iced tea and chatting about things both great and small. They enjoyed each other's company, and Seth perceived that a solid friendship was in the making. Lucci visited more often in the waning weeks, and the men often strolled through the woods or fished from the boat on Mirror Lake. Seth had a strong inclination that Lucci was still going to be part of his life; no mater what Eva would tell him.

Tiller had no desire to visit the underwater cavern. He hadn't seen Ariel or Aunt Bea on the lake. As three months approached since Eva's departure; it wasn't the lake or its secret that mattered anymore, but the love he had for Eva. Above all the gifts given to him throughout his life; the greatest one that he received was a second chance to love again, or better, to *truly* love someone for the first time.

On the morning of Christmas Eve, Tiller chopped down a six foot fir tree in the woods, and brought it back to the cabin. He decorated it with fruit and nuts that he collected during his recent walks through the woods, as well as with popcorn, cookies, and other foods that he asked Lucci to pick up for him. The tree was left outside of the cabin for it was meant for the animals of Mirror Lake.

His work was finished by noon, and he sat on the porch admiring it. Storm was the first to approach the tree, and zoned in on the carrots that Tiller had added to the tree specifically for her. It wasn't long before the loons arrived to nibble on the popcorn strings that hung on the lowest boughs of the tree. His keen sense of hearing allowed him to pick up the crackle of twigs coming from the trail that led to the cabin. At first, fear passed through him for he imagined that it was the black bear, but then he thought that it could be Lucci making a special visit on Christmas Eve.

As he turned to look, he saw Eva standing on the other side of the porch! She dropped the suitcase held in one hand and a shopping bag that was filled with gifts wrapped with Christmas paper in the other. She ran toward him as he rose from the rocking chair, covered his face with a sweet bouquet of small abrupt kisses, and finally gave him one long passionate kiss on the lips. The couple hugged each other with tears rolling down both sides of their faces. It was the best Christmas present that Tiller had ever received. The couple moved indoors, and over a mug of hot chocolate Eva spoke about her mother's final days on earth and her peaceful death. They spoke often about Seth, and before she died, Eva told her mother what she had decided to do. Mrs. LoPresti was pleased by what her daughter had planned, and gave both Eva and Seth her blessing. Tears once again filled the couple's eyes, as Eva spoke about her mother's funeral and burial. Tiller made her smile when he told Eva that she probably was chosen as heaven's chief cook and cookie baker!

After Eva finished speaking about her mother, she began to talk more about her future . . . and Seth's. She started by saying she took the liberty of calling Lucci to inform him of her decision. He thanked her for thinking of him, and that he'd talk more about it at a later date. She finally told Tiller what she chose to do. In essence, she handed him the proverbial ball back, and it was his turn to run with it.

Eva told Seth that she wanted to spend the rest of her life with him, but *not* at Mirror Lake. She sold her mother's house. With that money and what her mother left her, Eva purchased a log cabin similar to the one on Mirror Lake, but larger and not as remote. It sat on another part of Dam Lake, and was only a few miles away. Eva put everything on the line in making the move, and hoped that Seth would agree to be part of *her* plan. She wanted to have a *normal* family, raise a lot of kids, and to grow old with him naturally. She didn't want to watch her children grow older than their father, and she didn't want to age while her husband didn't. Her point was well taken. Although she was a spiritual woman, she told Seth that she didn't believe that she was destined to be a new Eve, nor did she want to live the rest of her life in an underwater cavern that could well be explained by Science, as something else other than the new Garden of Eden.

Tiller had never in his wildest imagination expected this kind of response from Eva. He had surprised her by bringing her to Mirror Lake, yet she had shocked him by what she had just said. He could accept a scientific explanation of the new world for he didn't necessarily believe that Science contradicts Religion, but what about the mermaid, behemoth, and the miraculous power of the lake water? She said that this, too, could possibly be explained by Science.

Not to leave Tiller with a sense that she had no regard for the role of Divine Providence, she asked, "Who are we to doubt that God couldn't use Mirror Lake for His own purpose? A purpose that could redeem an entire race, gives one man a second chance in life, or brings two people together for a lifetime of happiness, love, and fulfillment." Tiller could see her point, and replied by echoing something that he had heard and read many times in his life, "That God sometimes works in strange and mysterious ways."

He needed no additional time to think about what Eva had laid on the table. He wanted to spend the rest of his life anywhere with Eva, but wanted her to be happy there, too. If she didn't want to live at Mirror Lake, it would be fine by him. He accepted her proposal, and sealed it with another kiss. He asked her to whom she'd rather marry—Adam or Seth Tiller. She replied, "I want to marry the Tiller who is standing right in front of me." With this being said, the two rose from the sofa, and gave each other a hug. It marked the unofficial end of Adam Tiller, and the beginning of Seth Tiller.

Seth needed Lucci's help to bring an end to Adam Tiller, so they put into effect the plan that had been drawn up months ago. Adam's lawyer, once being informed by his client's "accidental" death, began to make the legal maneuvers necessary to transfer all assets to his son. This would take a few days, so Lucci permitted them to stay at Mirror Lake for as long as they needed.

Some people might say that Seth and Eva were crazy for not wanting to start their life together in a perfect world, but they'd say that there is an abundance of good in our imperfect world. Besides, how can two imperfect people ever survive living in a perfect world? Isn't it the case that the world never really changes, but the people who live in it? Can't the world still be a paradise, and that all people need to do is to become the good people that they were created to be? It took two weeks to draw up and sign off on all the legalities that involved both the death of Adam Tiller and the birth of Seth Tiller. Lucci was there for Seth and Eva, and continued to be a good friend. He picked them up from the side of the road, and drove them to their new house on Dam Lake. Being able to share the secret of Mirror Lake with Seth and Eva made his life seem more bearable.

It wouldn't be too long before Seth and Eva married in a quaint chapel in their town, and settled down as *Mr. and Mrs. Seth Tiller*. Not only was Lucci given the honor of being Seth's best man at the wedding, he was also asked to be the Godfather of the Tiller's first son, Thomas, who was named after Lucci's own son. The Bible says that Thomas means *twin*. Lucci believed that he was given a second son to love and watch grow into a fine young man. Best of all, was knowing that he'd pass on before him; the way that it should be in life.

On January 1st, Seth and Eva left Mirror Lake forever, but what had happened there, would never be forgotten. It was the place, or better, the experience that made Adam Tiller a new man. It had, indeed, served an important purpose. It was the start of a new year for the once, unhappy and unfulfilled writer, but more importantly, it marked the beginning of a new life for both he and Eva. Seth was given a second chance to do things right, and Eva was given the man for whom she had always prayed. Yes, her mother was right after all. Seth and Eva were truly meant for each other.

A month after Seth and Eva's departure from Mirror Lake, an old washed-up Hollywood actress plagued with an addiction to prescription drugs, notices an ad in a travel magazine. It is for a log cabin that sits alone on a beautiful lake in a remote area of Wisconsin's northwoods. She needs to get away from a world that on one hand has brought her fame and fortune, but also a life of unhappiness and emptiness. She picks up her cell phone, dials the number in the ad, and speaks to a man named Michael Lucci. He invites her to come out and see the property. He promises that she will love it, and that she will leave *a different person*. She agrees to fly out on her private jet, and to meet him in two days.

Mirror Lake continues to live on.